Contents

For my friends Maura, Kate and Louisa

Thank you for all your friendship, support and encouragement over the years!

IN THE
SHADOW
OF THE
EYE

Chapter 1

"Someone tried to murder me in broad daylight!" I moaned and mopped a trace of blood from my forehead. There was a blinding flash of pain in my neck and the back of my head. I felt a small trickle of blood down the side of my head. I staggered to my feet and with Ralph's help moved about unsteadily. I leaned over the balcony. Ralph had his arm around my shoulder.

"Take it easy Kevin," he said. There was a cool breeze coming up from the river which brought a little relief. I was scared. For the first time in my life I felt real fear. It could have been my life. My whole body was feeling weak and I couldn't move my head.

"Can I get you any help?" Ralph asked.

"Yes, would you phone the police and also Helen, my girlfriend?" I dictated the number as he dialled.

My head was throbbing with pain. When I could move again, I hunched over the rail in an effort to ease the pressure. Slowly I tested my limbs. Nothing broken! Then I shuddered as I heard footsteps coming towards me. This time I was on the alert but it was Helen.

"My God, what happened?" I just stood there in a stupor with my head on her shoulder. Ralph talked about the attack.

"I think you need to go to A&E," he said.

There was a sharp pain in my ears as they led me down the stairs and as I reached up I could feel more blood running down the side of my face. I began to cough feeling I might be sick.

When we arrived at casualty, a young doctor took me through into a cubicle right away. I seemed to have some of the most common symptoms of concussion; headache, slight dizziness and loss of balance. But the doctor quickly assessed that my brain was still functioning. I was aware of my surroundings and there seemed to be no difficulties with memory, or disturbances with vision such as seeing stars or flashing lights. He shone a light in my eyes.

"I'm satisfied that there are no serious symptoms of concussion," he said. "But we need to give you a precautionary X-ray and I would like you to see your GP tomorrow." He looked across at Helen and Ralph. "If you see any further signs of drowsiness or if he has severe headaches, take him down to causality immediately.

That was six years ago. College days were well-behind me and I had done a stint in the family law firm but I had now lost all that. Here I was in this strange place. I awoke with a jerk from my fuzzy dream. As Jock got nearer, his raucous singing became deafening. The dirty, jean-clad legs and the stifling smell of stale urine wafted over my nose.

"*Show me the way to go home, I'm tired and I want to go to bed. I had a little drink about an hour ago, and its gone right to my head.*"

"Quiet!" I shouted, angry and frustrated. It was a cold March day in 2005, my first week on the streets, or maybe I had been here for weeks or months, one more individual living on the margins of society. I had been falling helplessly into sleep. My dreaming mind conjured visions of childhood, parties, holidays abroad, romantic nights with Helen and I could now feel my whole body aching. In strange dreams; sometimes I saw my mother's face smiling down at me. Suddenly her face would turn into Rosemary's, my dear old Nanny, singing softly, taking me back to the nursery on the sunny days of my childhood. It was a strange kind of sleep full of dreams or more accurately hallucinations. I felt the tears sting my cheeks and could not help the spasm of nervousness that broke through my numb thoughts.

I was at Helen's funeral. Nothing could ever be the right way up again. The ground was gone from under my feet and I was tumbling into a darkness and a madness, suspended on the very edge of existence. The door to my real self and my real life had slammed shut. Fear, dread and confusion overwhelmed me. I was overcome with the most severe depression and the only solution was to end it all, put myself out of my misery. I had collapsed emotionally and had cast myself into the cold world of the homeless.

"No one prepares us," I thought, "for the unfair things fate throws at us and how fate makes us take stock of the mysteries of life and death." But there could be no solitude in this place. My inner thoughts were once more disturbed by Jock's rowdy singing. "*Wherever I may roam, over land or sea or foam...*"

"Be quiet," I yelled.

"*You will always hear me singing this song: Show me the way to go home.*"

"That's enough. Get to bed."

I often came under fire from Jock's erratic temper. He had sunk deeply into the habits of alcohol. The craving had ruled his life and tonight he had come slipping, tripping along the path with a beer in his hand slopping down his coat. Anger seeped through my body. I had experienced violence from my brother but tried never to show violence to others. I knew what it felt like to be bullied. I didn't want others to feel like I did.

A large cardboard box blocked the entrance. This was the front door, to mark boundaries for a living space. I noticed for the first time the glint of a gold ring on Jock's finger reflecting the gold of the beer. He had never talked about his previous life but I knew that everyone here had a story. After staggering around and finishing his beer, he flopped down onto his pillow of dirty newspapers and covered himself with the filthy sleeping bag.

Sometimes I had shared my space with heroin and crack addicts. The road which led some of them to living on the streets stretched all the way back to their childhoods and their relationships with their families. But my life had been different. I had been successful, had never missed a day off work, was extremely satisfied with my life and optimistic about the future.

"I was the luckiest man on the planet. No one in the world could have been happier," I thought and that feeling had stayed with me, and suffused every minute and every day of my existence right up until the day when my world fell apart. That was the last time Helen and I spoke with each other, the last time I saw her. A battle was raging within, my inner voice running over the events of that fatal day.

In the blink of any eye, my life had changed beyond recognition. Everything I knew and loved was ripped away in a sudden and random act of fate. In the semi-darkness a great yearning overwhelmed me. I felt the weight of all the memories, all the longings and all the shattered hopes and dreams. Abandoning my comfortable life I had buried myself in this murky world. There was a 'before' and an 'after', a brief moment when, abruptly, one life ended and another began. Fate dealt a cruel blow.

That tragic night was one of the lowest ebbs of my life. Only a dim corner of my mind was functioning, moving around in lurches, forward and back and becoming increasingly introverted. I felt weak and scared of everything; myself, my thoughts and any form of social contact, unable to confront my problems. I had always regarded homelessness with contempt. Yes I had dropped the odd copper into filthy caps but avoided any other contact, but restless and dislocated this had now become my passport out of a life of guilt, a place to hide my shame and embarrassment.

In happier days, Helen and I had always had our favourite spot in London, a city steeped in history but where best to find it than on the banks of the Thames. This was our favourite corner. We would walk by the river and discover the London of the twenty-first century and had already decided that the most dramatic sights were here along the embankment which is at the centre of the city's glorious history and backdrop for the evening news and the TV studios. We had always been attracted to the South Bank's splendour, its stormy skies or the quiet waters of this mysterious river. And now, as I lay on the cold cardboard, in the shadow of the London Eye, I felt that Helen had drawn me back to this place.

Alternating between despair and anger I felt it would be nice to go to sleep and never have to wake up again. I was wrestling with my conscience, terrified of what lay ahead and my mind refused to grasp any sense of reality. I was overwhelmed by a numbing kind of disbelief and I wanted everything to turn itself inside out and back to that day before the nightmare began. Death would be preferable to this living hell.

Chapter 2

Lightning flashed before my eyes. As they lowered my father's body into the grave the rain poured down in torrents. Under a huge umbrella, Mother and I held each other in a sobbing embrace as the vicar sprinkled some earth down onto the coffin.

"Come Mother," I took her arm and led her back to the black limousine. There was a further flash of fork lightning over the enormous oak tree which had stood in the cemetery for over a thousand years. I clung to mother and could feel the wet tears on both our faces but could do nothing to wipe either hers of mine away. She too was in a desperate state of trauma. The tragedy had pushed through the boundaries of reality.

"What am I going to do Kevin? It broke Reg's heart, Martin's sudden disappearance, not a trace left behind."

"It broke all our hearts Mother. After all he was my big brother, two years older, and he had always promised to look out for me."

"But no closure. The police drew a blank. We were just left in a limbo not knowing if he had run away, or if we would ever see him again.... and now your father has died of a broken heart."

"And what about Helen?" I interrupted. "There certainly was closure in her case," I paused, "I have always blamed myself."

She put her arm around me. "But you can't blame yourself. There was nothing you could have done. Why don't you come home Kevin?" she squeezed my hand. "I don't even know where you live. If it wasn't for Richard, you would never have known about your father's death."

"Richard has been a loyal friend to me and at this moment in time he is the only one I can trust."

"Does that mean you can't trust me?"

"Sorry Mother. I didn't mean that."

"But Kevin, if I could only have an address.... a phone number."

"Mother, I don't have a phone right now and the address is not permanent but don't trouble yourself. Things will change, but in the meantime you know you can always reach me through Richard."

"I know Kevin but I am not getting any younger. I have lost your Dad and my two boys. I loved you both equally. Martin knew that."

"Of course we both knew that," I said. But inwardly I wasn't too sure that Martin would have seen it that way. There were no grounds for jealousy but Martin had always considered himself to be the black sheep of the family. No one really knew Martin. I could still see the glint in my brother's eyes, something cold and triumphant, and the permanent mocking smile on his face. Sometimes when I heard Martin's laugh, I was scared to turn and face him. I could still hear him chuckle softly, an evil snigger. He liked humiliating me, trying to make me feel small. I remembered a time when he threw me to the ground, pressed down so hard that I could barely take a breath. Even as young as I was, I knew that there was something wrong with the way Martin got pleasure from hurting me. I remembered all the secret cruelties in my young life. There was a hardness about him that I found frightening. I could see it in his eyes. When we got older, the girls all thought Martin handsome, but no one stayed very long with him. It seemed to me that his cruelty was there for the world to see in that hard face and those watchful eyes and the voice that still tormented me. Even now, after all this time, I was flushed with high emotion. It wasn't even so much what Martin did, but what he was capable of.

"Kevin, are you there?" Mother asked.

"Sorry, I was miles away. You haven't lost *me*. I'm always a phone call away."

"But phoning Richard is not the same." I couldn't tell her that I had been living on the streets for over eight months. She would worry herself sick on top of all the concerns she had for my brother. That was the first day Richard had visited me in the cardboard and I knew something was seriously wrong with mother or father or maybe there was some news about Martin after all this time. When I heard of father's death I knew I had to make the effort to attend the funeral and with Richard's help, here I was.

The rest of that day was difficult. I met a lot of relatives and old friends, some I hadn't seen in years. There were awkward questions.

Uncle Dave came over and took my hand warmly. "It's a sad day for all of us," he said.

"Why don't you come back into the law firm where you belong? And now that your father has gone we need you. You know all this will be yours one day."

I knew that my uncle had a good idea of what had happened in my life. He was a shrewd man and there wasn't much that escaped his notice.

"We miss you Kevin," he put his arm around my shoulders.

"Thank you," I whispered but I was far away down the corridors of memory, drifting out of reach and didn't try to haul myself back.

I then moved back towards Mother.

"Are you okay Mother?" I held her for a moment after most of the guests had left. I just wanted to get away. There were too many painful memories. "Aunt Joan said she will stay with you for as long as you need her. I wouldn't be much company for you right now but I promise I will phone as often as I can."

Richard, who lived in a small basement flat about five minutes walk from the South Bank, was my one and only true friend and tried to understand in a non-judgement way that I had made a conscious choice to take time out.

"Here, you take the key of my flat," Richard said. "I will be there if you ever need a shoulder to cry on. And the most important thing to remember is that this is not the way the rest of your life is going to go. I will always be here for you and one day it will be like old times, believe me!"

Richard was my only link with the past. We had lived next door to each other in Derbyshire, started school together on our first day, had remained best friends right through to the sixth form. Although we had gone to separate universities, we had always remained close friend. The flat would just be a place to store my violin, guitar and my passport, my only possessions and maybe to keep my money box if there was anything left after the meagre scrapings from living on the streets. But I was determined to go there only when Richard was out at work. I would not take advantage of our friendship.

"I won't drag Richard any further into my own despicable life," I thought.

Not many people other than Richard knew of my predicament but those who did accused me of being selfish and reminded me of all the opportunities my parents had given me. I knew that I was not in the position of the 'normal' homeless person and tortured myself with recriminations and self-guilt.

Later that day, back in London when I walked along the embankment, the wounds of guilt pressed down on top of me. I had been possessed for years by these recurrent dreams of my brother's disappearance, a mystery still unsolved and then there was Helen's death. The currents in the river were pushing in opposite directions. For millions of years the Thames flowed towards the sea, washed up driftwood from faraway places on its journey, bobbing up and down on the river, each little piece of driftwood carrying its own story of its overwhelming journey.

I was just another piece of driftwood, unknown and unnoticed, swept along in the raging currents. I had put my whole life in jeopardy, and somehow I felt victimised and helpless. At this juncture of my life some outside force was exerting power over me and my only choice was to surrender, with my back to the wall. I was hungry and ate the last piece of bread. There was nothing to drink because I had finished the Coke earlier. I felt the sick taste in my mouth as though I was being suffocated, a familiar, frightening sensation that came back from the past to take me over. As I slumped down on my mat, Big Ben sounded out the hour, eleven o'clock. Life was now passing me by. Jagged memories jostled their way through my brain and this is where I would stay indefinitely. The blotches on my life were less visible in this life of grime, in this shapeless, threatening world of broken people.

The atmosphere was tense. No one had enough private space. With all the bridges and pavements in London, I wondered why a group of about six people had started to clutter up in this restricted space. Was it because of a need for security that some slept in little communities? Or was it a craving for family life? The surroundings looked dirty and dilapidated. I was just one more member of a sizeable homeless population. Apparently there were over five thousand official homeless in London, maybe more and many of the homeless had become prey to the city's drug subculture.

Jock had now turned over on his makeshift bed and his singing turned to a noisy, restless sleep. Glimpses of The London Eye could be seen through the delicate branches of the riverside trees. The Eye moved round and round relentlessly. My own life was going round and round and getting nowhere. Part of me believed the past was something to be left behind although my father had told me not to look back at past mistakes.

"Always look forward," was his catchphrase.

But a part of me was stuck in the past and memories prevented me from moving on.

Trains were coming and going at Waterloo station and it didn't matter if people were coming into London for a night out, or heading home to their cosy fires, I was still stuck there under the arches, going nowhere and with nothing to look forward to. I had left a job which millions would have envied and an income that most people would have been proud of. Despite the noises of trains and cars and snores, I finally dozed off but was too scared to sleep soundly.

The days drifted by endlessly and slowly, very slowly, it inched towards the Christmas season. I struggled to keep my darkest thoughts at bay. My first Christmas on the streets approached bringing freezing weather. I was feeling totally cut off from the rest of society which was not a position that I relished. I had always been strongly attached to my home and family and missed being with them at this time of year. Taxis and cars were whizzing by and the pavements were teeming with people, many of them loaded down with bags of Christmas shopping. Christmas advertised itself on every street and seemed to preoccupy every mind. I saw its daze and worry everywhere in people's eyes. Walking around the chivvying crowds and the slow moving buses staring at the brightness of everything, I asked myself over and over, "What's the point of it when life takes everything away?"

Police cars shimmered by, lit up by blazing lights and shrieking sirens. Ambulances could be heard accelerating through the traffic lights pushing everything out of the way.

A freezing wind was howling through the streets and across the river. Christmas lights flickered and swung in the rising winds of the dark afternoon. I sat hunched inside my worn coat with my hands deep in my pockets and collar pulled over my neck and I saw in their attitudes, that I was regarded by other people with terror and disgust. It just underlined to me how lost I was. Little groups of homeless people huddled down for the night, hiding themselves away in alleyways. Ragged people with nowhere to go. It was not yet dark but the lights were fading and the air growing colder. In the silence of the night the feeling of dread returned to me.

But at this point, Kevin was not aware of the strange figure with watchful eyes, the phantom of the night, tall and dressed in a long black coat and a hat covering his face, standing leaning over the metal rails of Hungerford Bridge and gazing towards the cardboard.

Chapter 3

My life had reached rock bottom. Everything seemed stuck in time. I was living like a beggar and totally disoriented, basically wasting my life away, with waves of bitter frustration running through my mind and hitting every nerve in my body. This period of my life had lasted for over a year in a fog of hopelessness. I had disappeared off the face of the earth. All my pride was gone and I didn't care. The months had been masked with a terrible depression clouding over me. I didn't like to catch sight of my own reflection in mirrors or doorways because what I always saw was my own misery at still being alive after the guilt of causing Helen's death. Others could chase the shadows away with drink and drugs, but my days passed in a monotonous blur, a jumble of contradictions. Now all I could feel was the burden of my exhausted frame sitting in the cardboard with the great unimaginable weight of the city around me.

My paranoia was at an all-time high and my hands were still shaking from outbursts of grief. I just walked around, haunted by my fears, chattering to myself, skulking through life, moving about in a daze. Those days and weeks and months will always be a blur. Looking back I find it hard to understand how I could have gone on like this for so long. The swirl of memory and emotion, of heartbreak and confusion, had worn me down and all I could do was hide in the shadows. Scared, cornered, trapped.

Suddenly there was a defining moment in my life, a gnawing need in me for all this to end. I was beginning to make a breakthrough. In the still semi-darkness a great yearning overwhelmed me. There was a brief moment when abruptly I asked myself, "What am I doing here?" My subconscious started fighting a battle of wills. Somewhere inside my head I could feel a sudden need to be proactive. Deep down I knew I couldn't carry on like this all my life and resolved to redeem my past or at least part of my past. Reproaching myself for my laziness and my thoughtlessness towards my family, a new wave of hope and ambition started to edge into my consciousness. I could only imagine that my mother must have been going through hell. At my father's funeral, I got an inkling of the grief I was causing her and knew she was desperately trying to find out where I was. Another prodigal son! And still no clues as to whether Martin was dead or alive. I now felt I owed it to my mother, to my Uncle Dave and also to Rosemary my dear old Nanny to at least start to reconstruct a vestige of what it was to live like a family again.

Of course one of the toughest things that I really did miss was the stimulation and challenges of work. My job had been stressful at times but I had enjoyed the professionalism and warmth of so many of my colleagues, especially the good social life and the many laughs we had together. Left to its own devices, my mind was caught in a constant struggle between optimism and pessimism. Days had merged into nights, weeks into months. But sometimes, just sometimes I got a glimpse of a future that would eclipse the present and renew me with a vision of hope.

"There's a world out there," I thought. "A world I should be re-engaging in, one that perhaps could comfort me a little, or distract me. Something significant in me had changed. Something fundamental. Things started to stabilise and I began to emerge from the shadows. It was then that it finally dawned on me with real clarity that I was going to survive. I had tried to focus once again on life and to concentrate all my efforts on resisting depression and trying to think positively.

"If I could only hang on and not lose heart," I kept telling myself. All I understood was that I had to try to rise up, to get free, to resume my journey. I crawled out of my hiding place and stumbled over towards the public toilets. My face looked ghostly, barely human in the cracked mirror. I turned on a tap and splashed water over my unshaved face. There was no light in my eyes. All around me I felt the pulse of the city beat faster as people gathered themselves for the working day.

I missed having a reason to get up early, a purpose to my day and most of the time I was heartbreakingly alone.

"Having abandoned my comfortable life and buried myself in my guilt, how was I ever going to hold my head up again?" For the first time in over a year, I began to reflect on my position from a different angle. A kind of panic clutched at me then. I could see people laughing and car doors slamming, the click of women's high heels on the pavement and men in city suits. I once had this kind of proper life.

Through that terrible first year, Jock despite his own problems and in a strange ironic way had been my saviour, had kept me alive by dragging me along to the Shelter for a little food and warmth. I have only vague recollections of that first day he took me in out of the cold. Cars were already screeching their brakes at the traffic lights outside the cardboard and an ambulance's siren blared through, with its blue lights flashing. Jock crept from under his coat and filthy sleeping bag, rubbing his eyes, his thin legs quivering as he stumbled to find his bearings.

"Come on lad." A wizened hand crabbed my wrist, gripping it with fearsome force. "You'll die of cold and starvation." I had moved into an alien environment where anything might happen and I was totally unaware of my own vulnerability. But Jock was streetwise. It seemed strange that this wizened old man, who had caused me so much irritation, had now come to rescue me. Shivering in the icy cold wind with my arms wrapped protectively across my chest, I just followed like a helpless toddler behind a trusting parent, my head lowered against the bitter wind.

When we reached the tall building, he started groping his way down the metal steps leading to the cellar below ground, hanging on to the handrail and feeling for the next step with his unsteady feet. His hands held onto the rail in a helpless way. He shuffled slowly and once or twice almost missed his step. This was a drop-in centre that cooked meals and provided somewhere for people to socialise for an hour or two, where they could wash, get a change of clothes and medical help or counselling when necessary. It was in a basement area almost hidden under the pavement, a warm place on a cold day and the only place that offered a welcome for dirty, dishevelled layabouts like myself who spent so much time in our sleeping bags or begging outside tube stations. It was the only place that offered any protection and respite from the cold world outside. No questions asked.

I slouched into a corner as far away from everyone as possible, just glad of the warmth to be found inside. Someone placed hot food and a steaming mug of tea in front of me, but I was so self-conscious wearing filthy clothes, unshaven, dirty hair greasy coat, confused and mumbling my thanks with my eyes looking shamefully at the floor. I was too consumed with all the pain, the want, the emotions, the deep hurt and the loss of Helen.

What I didn't know at this time was that I would eventually be picked up off the streets by the loyalty, love and respect from my friend Richard and the workers in the Shelter who all helped, provide me with the backbone to survive. But it was more than mere survival. As I slipped in and out of a weird, hallucinatory universe these were my liberators who would redeem me and guide me back along the road to reality. If only I could have had a glimpse of the bright future ahead! I wondered if it would get better. But it would, a lot better than I could possibly have imagined. My world would be different and a lot sooner than I thought.

I remembered Richard's words when I had taken him into my confidence and appreciated his offer to keep my few treasured possessions. At that time he had offered his support and made no judgements. He pleaded with me.

"You know I have a spare room here and it's yours for as long as you want. I know you Kevin. You have just lost your way for a while, but you are a fighter. Things will work out for you in the end."

That was all he said but I thanked him and declined his generous offer. I was determined not to involve him in my helpless situation. I didn't want anything to jeopardise our life-long friendship.

For the first time in over a year, I used Richard's key and retrieved my guitar. It was early afternoon as I headed off. I had a sudden lightness of heart. It was cold but I walked briskly down the street and over the bridge bounding up the steps with some new lyrics forming in my head. I was just relieved to be outside and away from the shadows that had become my prison. At that moment, I felt the need to gain a little independence and try to restore my dignity. At least there was now something reliable in my life, something that had a little meaning and a sense of purpose. I took off my jacket, opened up my guitar case and got ready to tune up. As the morning turned into the early afternoon, the crowds began to thicken.

Although I had been bitterly depressed and very fragile the night before, my music gave me the incentive to escape from my prison. This particular morning I was busking along the South Bank aiming to please my audience with a popular song. *"Is this the way to Amarillo, Every night I've been hugging my pillow, Dreaming dreams of Amarillo, and sweet Marie who waits for me..."*

I clearly remember that first day. A little girl opened her small purse and approached quietly to put money in my guitar case but immediately she was snatched away by her mother who in a very loud voice told the whole street, "He will squander it on drink and drugs."

The little girl seemed confused and looked back over her shoulder as she was roughly dragged along the pavement. I smiled across at her, my eyes trying to say, "It's OK. It isn't your fault."

I was agitated and couldn't blame people for feeling the way they did when they saw a strong, healthy young man living on the coppers of strangers. Later that day I had my first encounter with verbal abuse. It began as dirty looks and odd causal comments and later became threatening. I was told to piss off and get a proper job. They didn't understand that I was actually working. Ironically I had not experienced any of this when I was a real beggar, sitting outside the station with a dirty cap on the pavement in front of me and pennies dribbling in. But now I was working and the whole world seemed against me but I remembered Richard's words, "You are strong. You will survive."

Despite the verbal abuse which to be honest was only from a handful of people, I was determined not to give up. This was something I had to live with.

"This is their problem, not mine," I thought. "I have a legal pitch for my busking. I am not breaking any laws."

My music seemed to be back on form but my muscles which had taken a lifetime to build up through my rugby, steady exercise and athletics were already rapidly wasting away. My Father thought so highly of education and sports. At times he had been a hard and exacting father, but always loving and proud of his boys. He liked routine. From an early age I had started to thrive on stability and predictability. I now started my daily running sessions and began to see a sort of routine in it, up the steps, across Hungerford Bridge, picking up speed and trying to work things out. There was a vein of stern discipline running through me again. At this point, I started to run in the early mornings and found this energising. I could see the way my life had gathered momentum. I had made a bid for a new beginning.

Hope kept driving me on from day to day and my instinct for survival helped me believe that things would absolutely have to improve sooner or later. Somewhere inside I found the dedication and determination each day to continue. Life was different now. My running and my music were outlets for my anger and aggression. A new sense of achievement was creeping into my life. The transformation was small to begin with but I started to see life a lot more clearly and I could almost feel some of the anger and paranoia falling away.

A new era had begun and this time it was going to last.

It was now over a year since I had arrived on the streets and I had clearly begun to emerge from the shadows that had been lurking around me and that had almost claimed me. Deep down, I now knew that for me there could really be nothing worse than never escaping from that kind of prison. I surprised myself with the way I adapted to the new demands. Now I had changed. Over the next month I just hung in there, relaxing, recovering and rebooting myself. Life had settled into a real routine. Each morning I would get up trying desperately to straighten myself out. Guilt had crushed me but I had picked up the pieces, put myself back together and moved on with my life. I couldn't do enough to escape the horrible shadows. It felt like the most enormous triumph over fate and the need to continue became an imperative. To restore my existence, I realised that I finally had to take control over my life again. I had turned some sort of corner but I wasn't sure yet where it was leading.

But as Kevin returned to the cardboard that evening, a mysterious figure stood on the bridge, dressed in a long black coat, a baseball cap pulled down over his face, holding a cigarette in his left hand, lighting up the darkness on the bridge. The spark of light glowed in the shadows, like a tiny eye, watching, all-seeing, peering into the gloom.

Chapter 4

The following days, weeks and months will always be a blur. Days passed, weeks passed and winter had come and gone again. Big Ben had just struck eight when Jock crept from under his filthy sleeping bag in the cardboard. He raised himself up on one elbow rubbing his eyes, his thin legs quivering as he gripped onto the side of the wall to try and steady himself. He was a lot worse for the wear from the previous night on the booze.

"I'm off to the Shelter for a hot cup of tea. Come on lad?" he said as I helped lift him to his feet. I no longer wanted to remain a frustrated loner on the outside. I had started to free myself from the frustrations and neurosis that pushed me into solitude. In the beginning I was reluctant to take any hand-outs but I knew the help was there if only I could accept it. I tugged up the collar of my jacket as a slight drizzle began to fall and I walked towards Westminster under the pretences, in my own mind, that I was supporting Jock but deep down I knew I was beginning to take on a new life. As we walked down the steps to the Shelter in the basement area, almost hidden under the pavement, Jock was carefully holding on to the iron rails.

We entered through a long corridor. I stopped. Suddenly I saw the notices on the doors: Toilets, Showers, Office, Library and Clothing Store. I was impressed by all the facilities. For over a year I had been coming here just walking in like a zombie, head bowed, moving in a clumsy slouching way, grabbing some hot food and disappearing back outside onto the hostile streets. Most of the time I spent in a stupor, sitting, walking, shuffling around.

"Nothing like the smell of fried bacon," Jock said as we went through to the warm dining room where the pleasant aroma of grilled food, coffee and toast greeted our nostrils.

Already less disorientated, I stopped in my tracks. This place was somehow different now. I had drifted into the Shelter so many times but until that day I hadn't seen the faces of any of the volunteers, just kind hands putting warm food on my plate. The first person I saw was Kate. I suddenly became conscious of my being pale and unshaven, staring shamefully at the floor, in my cast-off clothes and worn out shoes and had tried to avoid meeting peoples gaze.

"My God, what must they have thought of me?" I wondered. I didn't like to catch sight of my own reflection in mirrors or doorways because what I always saw was my own guilt at still being alive.

Someone behind the counter was calling Kate's name. Her long blonde hair was tied back neatly in a ponytail which swished back and forth as she walked briskly around the tables. These were real people with faces and names. There were six volunteers, six smiling faces but Kate was the one who captured my attention. She was unassuming and yet efficient as she moved lightly between the tables. But there was something nervous in her bearing like she was a bit scared if one of the men approached to ask her for help.

For the first time, I went to the hatch and served myself with some bacon and egg, crusty bread and a large mug of coffee. As I was about to pick up my tray, Kate walked towards me with a smile.

"Welcome Kevin," she said but there was something about her that made her hold back. How did she know my name? I felt stupid and awkward, yet I saw that she wasn't irritated. I thanked her but in my embarrassment my old inhibitions were coming back and I was conscious of my dirty, ragged coat and my scruffy appearance. I had hauled myself up and stumbled along the street, living from hand to mouth.

My face looked pale and ghostly, barely human. There was no light in my eyes. For the first time I felt everyone was studying me and feeling sorry for me. I held my head down in embarrassment, suddenly self-conscious, aware that I could do with a good shave and a change of clothes. But Kate seemed unaware of my clumsiness. She went around serving everyone, chatting in a quiet way as she went, greeting people by name as she rushed around carrying out her duties. This place provided me with a little bit of warmth and friendliness in my otherwise frantic impersonal life.

There was a genuine, warm-hearted welcome. Strange I hadn't noticed it before. I tried to make myself as inconspicuous as possible, looking for a little solitude in the crowded room. I walked to the furthest corner, squashed myself into an uncomfortable huddle and sat there awkwardly, staring blankly at my plate, my hand shaking as I drank my coffee and planning a hasty retreat but I realised now that this was the only place that offered any protection from the cold world outside. But on my way out I saw an older lady with 'Supervisor' on her badge.

"Welcome to the Shelter. My name's Maura," she said as she held out her hand. I felt the warmth of her handshake, as something comforting, in fact the only real comfort I had received since coming on the streets.

"I'm Kevin." I was amazed to hear the sound of my own voice. Maura had made me feel completely at ease. She seemed like a sort of surrogate mother and had helped lift my embarrassment.

I asked about the showers and the clothes store, still conscious of my filthy appearance, unshaved, greasy hair, ragged clothes and confused mumblings.

"You can shower anytime you like. We have everything in there, soaps, gels and towels and you can have a shave if you like." This embarrassed me. I could feel her gazing at my scruffy appearance.

"I can get you your own shaver."

I was unable to answer for a moment and just looked down at the floor. Then she invited me into her small office. Away from the crowded dining groom I began to regain my composure.

Suddenly I was speaking again. Speaking to another human being. "You are so kind to give your time to listen to all these people, all our tales of woe."

"No, believe me, there are not many who want to talk. I have plenty of time. No great demands from the others. Most people just want to get into the warmth out of the cold streets and get a warm breakfast inside them and who can blame them. It must be cold out there. I just wanted you to know that we are here to help. As well as providing warm food on a cold day, we are also here to listen. You know we have a doctor who comes here once a week and I can make an appointment for you if you would like to see him."

"No! No!" I said. The trembling and shaking began. There was tightness in my chest. Suddenly I felt all the wind go out of me as if I might faint or burst into tears. "Count to ten," I told myself, trying to remain calm holding tightly onto the arm of the chair. After a little while, I had regained some self-control, enough to speak calmly again. "The doctors only want to pump me with antidepressants. I need to sort this out in my own way." These panic attacks came on at the most obscure times, sometimes unexpectedly. I felt the briefest moment of trepidation and my hand reached out again to steady myself.

Seeing my distress, Maura waited patiently until I lifted my head. "It's ok. Sorry it was only a suggestion. I won't mention doctors again. Everyone who comes here has their own story of love and loss, maybe partners struggling to cope with a disabled spouse. There can be heartbreak and despair everywhere," Maura said gently. There was a kindness in her tone but no pity. It was obvious that she was trying to keep hope alive in me.

I was still dizzy with a pounding in my chest but began to take comfort from Maura's words and the safety of this quiet space. Maura handed me a glass of water. "Here, just sit quietly and it will pass." It was clear to her that I had been suffering from some sort of post-traumatic stress.

"I'm ok now, sorry about that outburst," I said. Maura had a calming effect on me. She reminded me so much of Rosemary, my dear old Nanny. Rosemary always knew how to calm me especially when she knew Martin had been bullying me.

"So you have come back to us," Maura said. "I have been watching you for over a year now and I knew you were going to make it in the end." I was silent for a moment. I just sat there wondering what people had thought of me for all this time. I instantly knew that Maura was a person I could trust. There weren't any people in my situation I could talk with and very few who wanted to listen. Suddenly I wanted to explain my situation, to tell her everything.

"There was one particular day," I told her, "when quite abruptly my life ended and another one began, my new life here on the streets. I had a beautiful fiancée, Helen," I paused and could feel the tears welling up in my eyes. I was desperately trying to hold myself together.

"It's okay. Let it all come out," the light fell briefly on her face as she spoke. "You need to talk but don't go on if you find it too painful. You can always come back another time." Tears were choking me and I pressed a tissue to my face.

"In the week before my wedding, my life changed forever, something that no one could possibly have foreseen, a sudden tragedy. I was twenty-nine, the same age as Helen. At weekends we went to the pub or to the cinema, just like any other young couple. In the summer we often went down to a beach in Cornwall. Before the tragedy, I thought of myself as just a normal person, living a normal life. After Helen's death, I couldn't think clearly any more. My mind was foggy and I felt anger and guilt all the time." I went on and told her the whole story, about what had happened on that fatal day.

"The streets are alien territory for me. I am terrified. It's like I have stepped off a cliff into the unknown. This seemed quite simply the only way to go. Others can turn to drink and drugs for comfort but I haven't even tried. What's the point of it when life takes everything away."

"Everyone is right. It wasn't your fault. You mustn't go on blaming yourself," she said quietly. Are you listening?" She asked the questions with such sensitivity.

I nodded and murmured a "Yes."

Her voice was tender. She looked up at me. "Do you know anything about hope Kevin?" she asked. "The world is messy. Some people think it is black and white but it is full of grey areas. Loaded up with grey. We live in a murky world. Even those people you see in their smart city clothes. Then I'll tell you something good. Your life can and will turn around but of course you need to give it time. I have seen it before many times. But you don't have to let that last night with Helen be the thing that defines you."

There was a ray of sunshine coming from a small stain glass window at the top of the wall and Maura's silver hair glinted in the light as she went on speaking, "We are here for everyone, regardless of race, colour, gender or orientation, rich or poor," she hesitated. "Tragedy can strike at any level. It happens to normal people like you all the time. It could happen to me too."

I sat for a while without speaking and then in lower tones I said, "I know this is entirely my own making and mine to mend."

"Go easy on yourself. Try not to keep punishing yourself for something that was a genuine mistake, with tragic consequences, but a mistake nonetheless." I knew she was here to help, but I wasn't sure if I wanted any help. I sat for a while without speaking.

"There are very few situations in life that have to be faced alone," Maura was speaking softly again. It was the voice that was going to set me free. There was a sweetness in her nature that made her attentive to others.

"I feel weak and scared of everything, myself, my thoughts and any form of social contact. I am unable to confront my problem. I am too scared, too weak and incapable of doing so. It is controlling my mind too much for me to do anything about it," my hands were shaking as I spoke. We sat there for a while in silence.

"Thank you," I said at last. "There is no one else I could have told. I have a friend, Richard, who lives in this area. We grew up together and he is the only one who understands my situation but he has a demanding job as a barrister and I don't want to get him too involved. Anyhow I need to sort this out in my own way, in my own time." There was sweetness in her nature that made her a good listener, attentive to others.

"These people are amazing," I thought. "They look into broken, scarred, battered features, sometimes uneducated and simple-minded people or people like me who have fallen by the wayside and they see something that nobody in our lives has ever seen. They see fine men and women rather than a bunch of stinking, homeless layabouts."

Maura took my hand and led me gently out the door towards the showers. She showed me where everything was. When she had gone back to her little room, I stood under the hot water in the shower and felt that all my pain and suffering was being washed away. The feel of the warm water and the soap on my body was so soothing, I almost felt like crying. I scrubbed at my body until it was tingling and the stench was gone. After a long time, I stepped out and wrapped myself in the soft towels which were hanging on the rail. I put on the clean clothes which Maura had given me and ran a comb through my hair. My eyes were tired. I deliberately dressed very slowly relishing the feel of the warm clothes on my clean body. It's strange how a simple thing like a shower had an immediate impact on my life, like I had washed away all my sins. I had not shaved since arriving on the streets. My beard had been growing, hairy and free. I felt a new man in clean trousers, a thick sweater and warm socks.

When I returned to the dining room, I felt renewed in body and soul. I went to my usual corner, placed my head on the table and immediately dropped into the sleep of the innocent.

"Wake up sleepy head." It was Sr. Gabriel with a steaming cup of coffee and a plate of sandwiches. "Is that you Kevin or am I having an apparition?" she placed her arm around my shoulders. "Quite a handsome guy underneath all that grime," she laughed.

"Sorry Sister," I said.

"Nothing to be sorry for," she laughed.

This was another new beginning. My longing to be clean increased steadily from that day. Maura had made an attempt to see me as a person, still whole and intact. She was here to offer people some comfort, to help them on the road to a better life. But I soon discovered that these people would transform my future and have a profound effect on the rest of my life. I hadn't felt this good for over a year.

But I gasped as I noticed a strange figure over in the dimly-lit corner wearing a faded yellow sweatshirt. His hair and short beard almost looked like a disguise.

"Calm down," I told myself. "It couldn't be." My imagination was getting the better of me.

On leaving the dining room, Sr. Gabriel handed me a packet of sandwiches neatly wrapped in foil, and on my way down the corridor Maura called me over and gave me an anorak with a thick, fleecy lining. Such spontaneous acts of generosity hadn't exactly been a part of my life up until this moment. Thanks to Maura, I had rediscovered the good side of human nature. These were genuine, warm-hearted people, providing me with a little bit of light relief, a bit of warmth and friendliness in my otherwise frantic, impersonal life. I had begun to place my trust and faith in people again.

For the first time in over a year and a half, I felt like I could see the tiniest light at the end of a very dark tunnel. I realised that I was finally taking some control over my life again. I was being offered a second chance and I couldn't let it slip through my fingers.

Chapter 5

I was still panting from all the running I had done already that morning. There was a feeling of spring all over the city with white buds bursting from the blackthorn hedge along the embankment. I had hit rock bottom but now I had become concerned only with my own survival. The world had flown past with horrifying speed, past all those ordinary people who remained oblivious to the enormity of what was unfolding in my life. There was a stream of people flowing in and out to the station, talking and laughing and in some small way I began to see myself as one of those normal people with a future almost within my grasp. But for the moment time was suspended.

Full of the joys of Spring, I made my way to the Shelter and met Maura in the corridor. This time I was feeling a lot more positive. "I will take up your kind offer and have another shower if I may."

"Of course." I needn't tell you, there isn't a long queue at this time of the morning."

Left alone in the shower room, I felt like a new person. I could have stood there forever with the warm water giving me that long-lost feeling, Maura met me coming out of the showers. "Here, I have found you a nice warm blanket."

"Thanks, this is perfect," I bowed my head and tried to hide my embarrassment. "I really do appreciate all you are doing for me."

"You know I am always here if ever you want to talk," she said.

I thanked her and feeling quite hopeful and a lot cleaner, I ventured into the dining room.

But there was no Kate. I felt an emptiness which I couldn't explain and just slumped into a chair next to Jock. The other volunteers came over to see to all my needs.

"Oh bloody hell, you smell like a chemist's shop. What's all that muck on your hair?" Jock looked at me in disgust.

"I had a shower and it's only a bit of gel," Inwardly I thought that a good wash and some clean clothes wouldn't go amiss with poor old Jock.

"Why don't you get some more warm clothes from Maura and a blanket? They have everything in that store room."

"I have everything I need. Leave me alone lad. You do your thing and I'll do mine. That's a fair deal."

Sr. Gabriel came across with a plate of food and hot drink and placed it on the table in front of me.

"Glory be to God, is that yourself Kevin? I thought you were a member of that film crew who are making a documentary about the Shelter. Did you fall into a puddle on the way over?"

I smiled at her joke. "No Sister. I just went to the shower room and got some clean clothes from the store room!"

"Are you Irish?" she asked. "Me brother is called Kevin, a very popular name over in the auld country."

"Well no. I'm actually from Derbyshire. But my father had Irish ancestors so I guess that's how I got the name. Do you all come here every day?" I ventured to ask.

"Yes most of us. Well, all except Ellie and Kate. They are teachers and only come at the weekends." So that explained the mystery of the missing Kate. I don't know why I had singled her out and I began to look forward to seeing her again on Saturday.

Sister Gabriel was a tall, friendly nun, always in a cheerful mood. She went around jollying everyone up. I found out later that she was in her seventies, travelled from the East End by two busses and two trains every day of the year come rain or shine. Strangely I hadn't paid much attention to her before either. And I was also becoming more aware of Len, one of the street people like myself who kept everyone informed in the latest news, with his fund of knowledge, though not all of it good. A whole new world was opening up in front of me, a world full of real live people.

Len sat with a sandwich, cup of coffee and the newspaper spread out on the table. Reading the papers was a lengthy business for him. He liked to assimilate all the latest news and knew just about everything there was to know about politics and the social history of London. Today he talked about the hype of the press. The sensationalism! But I sat in a quiet corner trying to piece my own life together. I was a disgrace to the human race. "I didn't get to say goodbye to Helen," I had mulled this over and over in my mind. It was now well over a year since the tragedy. Yet in a way, since I had met Maura, I had taken on an air of quiet hopefulness.

"I am like an alien from another planet but nobody really bothers me," I thought.

"You have to grow up and act like a man," I told myself. Every part of my being had been ruled by my own misery but now I seemed to have woken up and to be yearning for warmth and friendship, for any crumbs of attention that came my way.

My mother had said our lives should make a difference to the world. So what went wrong? I shouldn't be a charity case. I had no right to rely on the help of other people. I knew in my heart that I had to get back my life, allow myself to accept responsibilities for it. I owed it to my mother and to myself.

"What is holding me back?" I had asked this question over and over.

Len continued to sit in the corner in his usual position by the small window, surveying the world from his own perspective.

"Things are not like they used to be" was his favourite saying.

"Pubs used to be small and cosy. Everyone knew everyone else and the barmaid always had a smile for everyone." Len had been in Australia for forty years. The one thing he looked forward to was a quiet English pub.

"I always loved a quiet pint in the old days and I couldn't wait to get back to the English beer and English pubs. But nowadays you can't even find a seat. There's pushing and shoving at the bar, silly girls shrieking in every corner. It's worse than Australia. The old folk used to tell stories over their pints and put the world to rights. It would take more than a pint to put the world to rights today."

Sister Gabriel floated over in our direction, her long black habit swishing between the tables.

"More coffee Kev?" I noticed she had shortened my name, probably in some form of endearment. Before I could answer, she whisked my mug off the table and returned with a steaming hot coffee and a Danish pastry.

"Thanks Sister," I said. "You are too kind."

"We must have a long chat sometime," she said and swished off to attend to everyone else's needs.

"And what about the countryside? That's another matter," Len was still pontificating. "There used to be larks and nightingales, cuckoos and a land of curlews and blue skies. All gone. Killed by insecticides and industrial farming! Now it's all cars and pollution." Most people found Len irritating but I often sat within earshot. A lot of what he said made sense. Occasionally I made some polite reply but decided to lose himself in books. This morning I had discovered the books in the Shelter and I knew there were book stalls along the Millennium Mile. I wanted to read and reread anything I could get my hands on.

"It's what I am best at," I thought. "Books, reading, the free newspapers, my music, my running. There isn't much else to do."

I had been trying to work out my repertoire for the afternoon's stint on my busking patch. A Bette Midler song was running through my mind as I went to pick up my guitar. I quickly tried to memorise the words, tuned up and decided to give it a go.

Some say love, it is a river, that drowns the tender reed...When the night has been too lonely, and the road has been too long, and you think that love is only for the lucky and the strong....

I had just finished my session and was packing up when I got a surprise to find Richard standing in front of me.

"That was brilliant, one of my favourite songs," he said. "I see you have taken on a new look. Why don't you come around the corner to one of those coffee bars and we can have a chat?"

We sat across the table like old times. This was the first time I had spoken with Richard for any length of time since I came on the streets. I told him about the difficulties of living on the edge, the risks and hardships but how my life was beginning to turn a corner.

"It's strange," I said. "I think I am almost ready to resume a proper life, to go back home, sort out my finances, take up Uncle Dave's offer to rejoin the law firm."

"But," he said. "There is a 'but', isn't there?"

"Good old Richard, my only true friend who knew me better than anyone else in the world. Astute as always," I thought.

"Well yes there is a big 'but'. If I return to the straight and narrow, I will lose contact with my friends at the Shelter. At the moment, they are my lifeline." I didn't tell him about my feelings for Kate. But in my heart I knew this was just infatuation. Our friendship couldn't really go anywhere. Anyhow I had only seen her once or twice at the weekends and there could be no future in this type of relationship.

"You are wise," he said. "Give yourself a little more time. There is no need to rush into anything just yet. Ok, so that's it. I will be back to listen again and next time we will make arrangements to have you over to dinner at my place. Here, give me the guitar. It will save you the walk."

"Thanks," I said and watched him stroll across the bridge, heavy briefcase in one hand and my large guitar case in the other. I thought of something Oprah Winfrey had said, "Lots of people want to ride with you in the limo, but what you want is someone who will take the bus with you when the limo breaks down." That was Richard! And William Butler Yeats had his own take on friendship, "Think where man's glory most begins and ends, and say my glory was I had such friends." I stood there counting my blessings, looking across the river and thinking of all the treasures in my life, Richard, my family and now my new friends at the Shelter.

But that night a dark figure hovered on the bridge gazing down towards the cardboard, standing arrogantly, unchallenged, certain of its own authority.

Chapter 6

In my nightmare the graveyard scene flashed into my mind, lightening and torrents of rain, thick black clouds low over our heads and my mother's loud sobs. I didn't want to have to deal with anyone at my father's funeral. I went so far as to lead my mother out a side door to avoid the crush of other family members and friends. Numbness crept in when the flow of people had stopped coming out of the chapel. Then in my mind there was the other funeral, a white hearse flashing before me, drawn by four white horses, a slow cortege, carrying my beloved Helen slowly, slowly on her last journey, the floral name reflecting through the glass side of the hearse, telling the world that this was her last goodbye. A shower of pink roses covered the slim, white coffin and I stood motionless with a single red rose in my hand.

In the early morning light my tears were now mingled with a light rain which had begun to fall gently on the pavement at my feet and I was still overcome with spasms of guilt. I had been responsible for Helen's death and had tasted the grief and anger. They told me anger was part of his grief process but time would heal. Time did not heal. I was the cause of Helen's death. Men were not supposed to cry or show emotion. I had cried. Did this make me a failure as a man and had I now become a poor specimen of humanity with my manhood dissolving into nothingness? I might have been able to accept the tragedy of sudden death but could not forgive myself for my selfishness on that fatal night.

It all flashed through my mind. Helen had called around in her jogging suit to show me the place settings for our wedding. She took a pebble from her pocket.

"You asked me why I was collecting all those beach pebbles last summer on holiday. Well now you know. Each pebble will have the name of a guest.

I saw my name written in deep purple, to match the wedding theme, surrounded by glitter and a little white dove in the corner. As I held it up it was reflected in the light.

"What a wonderful idea. Can I show this to my parents?"

"Yes, I hope they like it. You keep that one. It's only a sample for your approval. These pebbles have been around for millions of years and have weathered all the storms. Just think of waves lapping against the shore and in our own lives, breakers that crash over us. The sea is powerful, constant, unrelenting, and overwhelming. In the end, the sea always wins. In the end, it always triumphs!" I liked the way she had of describing things.

"Just like we will do," I laughed, "but there will be no storms in our relationship."

Helen was a dreamer, a bit of a poet and that was what had attracted me to her in the first place.

"I'm always suspicious of married people who say they have never had an argument, aren't you?" Helen looked up at me with her beautiful smiling face, the love sparkling in her eyes as she swept the long blond hair back behind her ear. There would never be anyone like her.

I held the pebble in my hand; as she reached down to kiss me for the last time.

"I should have gone with her," I had told myself over and over again. That was the last time I saw her alive.

At this point in time, I didn't seem to have the faintest idea what was right or wrong any more. I still had a sudden sense of dropping from a great height. Traffic screeched to a halt at the traffic lights which were right outside the cardboard and I began to shiver with the cold. I hadn't felt this cold before and thought it was numbness, but now it seemed to hit me at once, as if the wind was piercing right through my skin. My feet were aching with a cold that gnawed into my very bones. The reason for my despair was pure and simple, loneliness and depression. In this lifeless world, if a person wanted to stay in the shadows they could. But Jock in those early days had dragged me reluctantly to the Shelter.

I got through the tougher days because of my little garden, a small plot across from the cardboard. There seemed to be something miraculous about seeing the relentless optimism of new growth after the bleakness of winter, a kind of joy in the difference every year, the way nature chooses to show off different parts of the garden. The satisfaction of seeing things living and glowing in their temporary beauty captivated my imagination. The leaves here were thick and there was a large knot of brambles a few feet away. I busied myself, digging and weeding, cutting things down with new-found efficiency, watching the sunlight playing through the leaves. In the evening I stood there watching the sun sink fiery red over the Houses of Parliament. The sweet smell of the grass rose up around me. I looked across at my precious little garden which had begun to bloom, a pale melding of pinks, mauves and blues. I had begun to understand the consolations of doing something.

On one particular evening I strolled into the small park at the side of the station and watched the children pushing each other on some swings as their young mothers stood around chatting, dressed in light tops and jeans. Something new made me feel alert and fearless. I had acquired a new vision of London, a secret vision in this peaceful place. Suddenly there was alarm everywhere. When they saw me the parents called their children from the swings and had their arms round them in a protective way and I suddenly understood that they thought me some sort of a threat.

"He's not going. Someone, call the police!" one of the mothers grabbed a mobile phone from her daughter.

"It's alright," I said. "I was just leaving anyway." I turned on my heel and disappeared out the side gate towards the embankment but before I left, I heard one of the women say, "He's crazy. Some sort of weirdo."

This had been a big set-back for me. My self-esteem was really low. It had started plummeting again and here I was living back in the depths of this new alienation. I needed to be alone and often wondered how I could continue like this from day to day. Sometimes I was unable to disguise my despair but I knew there was always some comfort at the Shelter. I needed to find distractions to alleviate the tedium of this new life.

After breakfast at the Shelter I picked up my guitar and went across the bridge. The volume of people wasn't as great in the mornings but it became really busy in the late afternoon and evening with hundreds of tourists on the street heading to the West End cinemas and theatres. I was soon making a healthy profit. People from all around the world were milling around taking in the sights of central London, some with rucksacks, other clutching street maps, all looking a little overwhelmed at finding themselves at the beating heart of London.

A lot of people would stop and drop coins into my guitar case particularly a group of regulars, who worked in the area and liked my music. I spent hours most days playing the guitar, improving my songs. Just occasionally some people took exception to me, approaching me with disdain, and could be rude and even abusive at times.

But I knew in my heart that things would improve. I had got glimpses of a brighter future ahead for me and I hoped these feelings would return.

Chapter 7

The weekdays dragged but I found myself bright and early back at the Shelter on Saturday mornings. These were my favourite days and after the first few weeks I tried to unleash some of my shyness in Kate's company. But Kate herself seemed a little shy or nervous. This helped me in a way to feel a lot calmer.

On the first Saturday after I had met Maura and begun showering on a daily basis, I reached the dining room and was greeted by Kate.

"Good morning Kevin, you look different." She seemed a little less fragile now.

When my voice emerged, it was in a whispered "Good morning," and I still held my head down slightly embarrassed.

Kate wasn't wearing any make-up and later I noticed her nails were like tiny pink pearls, neatly manicured and I saw that there were no rings on her fingers. Her only piece of jewellery was a tiny cross on a gold chain around her neck and small gold studs in her ears. There was a simplicity about her which I found endearing but also a sadness. When I had finished Kate was at my side, removing the plates and cutlery.

"I hope you feel a bit warmer after that," she gave me a kindly smile but this only sent me further into myself.

I made an effort to sound casual but I hardly knew what I was saying. It wasn't in my nature to be tongue-tied but then I had never been in this situation before.

I didn't really feel like eating much but this was the day when I was determined to break the ice and venture more than a mumbled 'Thanks'.

Kate's fair hair was tied back with a checked ribbon and I noticed that her slim hands had a slight tremble as she handled the ladle trying to avoid any spills as she served porridge from a large cauldron.

"And how are things with you?" She continued to concentrate on the task in hand, already looking at the next customer.

"It's now or never," I thought.

"Do you do this every day?" I asked, although I already knew quite well that Saturday and Sunday mornings were her only shifts at the Shelter.

"Oh no. I'd like to but I am a teacher during the week.... for my sins," she gave a little smile.

When everyone was served Kate rushed around tidying up and clearing tables.

I thought, "Why should a pretty young girl who has such a demanding profession, give up her precious time to feed layabouts and lazy louts like me?" I felt embarrassed but Kate's cheerful approach lifted my spirits.

After our initial greetings, I still sat in a quiet spot away from the others. I got the feeling, or maybe it was wishful thinking, that Kate was watching me from the far side of the dining room, her face radiant, her hands forever in motion seeing to everyone else's needs. She had bright, intelligent eyes and there was an inquisitive smile on her face. My feelings were being drawn, slowly and inevitably toward her. I wanted to enter the realm of her world.

It took me a long time to understand the intensity of those feelings and so for a long time I pretended to myself that it wasn't love, just an infatuation for a beautiful young girl who gave so generously of her time to help wretches like myself. She had given me a different perspective on life and I was foolishly telling myself that maybe she could love me, that she needed and cared for me in some strange way. I was happy, no longer lonely, instead I felt curiously free. But living a dream.

I was still cautious and withdrawn, embarrassed in a way. The softness of Kate's tone did something to me and made me look around to where she was serving at the tables. Sometimes she looked straight back at me or maybe I was imagining it. I wanted to speak, to say something but somehow I couldn't get the words out.

The next day, the Sunday morning, Kate walked over to where I was sitting.

"Maura will get you some aspirin," she said. She had seen me holding my brow and it looked as though I might have a headache or a slight temperature.

"It's ok," I said. "I often got headaches, a side-effect, I think, of my anger and frustration and my misguided attempt to stay in control." Suddenly I found that I did have a voice after all. My confidence had returned and it astonished me.

"Why am I saying these things? Is this some sort of illusion?" I thought. "What could Kate see in me, a strong young man who should be out doing a decent job instead of living this way?"

There was a long silence, punctuated only by the clacking sound of chairs, and fast feet rushing around to help everyone.

"It's nice of you to take the trouble. It isn't everyone who would give up their time to wait on layabouts, a huddle of washouts like me."

"I don't want to pry and I hope you don't think me rude," Kate said, "but you don't seem the type for living rough," she said quietly, "but I can see there's something wrong or you wouldn't be here."

Taken by surprise, I stumbled over my words as I told her a little about the tragedies in my life and she listened to what I was telling her without butting in.

"I sometimes wonder myself why I am on the streets," I thought. "Maybe it's part of some big eternal plan. Maybe fate, maybe that's it."

But all I said was, "Do you believe in fate?"

"I don't really know. I hadn't given it much thought before. I just seemed to drift from school to University and then to work. Maybe it was predestined. Or I guess I was just lucky." That was it. There was a little shyness in her voice but then she had to move on with her duties.

"Take care," she looked back as she moved around the tables. I had to move on too.

"See you," she smiled over her shoulder. They were already closing the doors. I smiled back and then had to move towards the exit. Maybe if I lingered at the end there would be an opportunity to continue the conversation. But I had to keep going. The volunteers had started to clear everything away. There was no time for idle chat.

"Thank you," I continued to walk towards the door. That was it. I didn't think I had the right to accept this kind of charity and impose on the generosity of these volunteers. Maura has made me feel comfortable, almost at home. But with Kate it was different, I had been so embarrassed by my own appearance and my feelings, almost like some insecure teenager.

The table inside the door was laden with packs of sandwiches, some fruit and bottles of water to be taken away for later. I was embarrassed picking up supplies for the evening and hoped Kate wasn't watching. Once more I was attacked by feelings of guilt and selfishness. My life was a total disaster.

Kate had a strange effect on me although I felt that she was vulnerable in some way and lacked confidence. I lay awake thinking about her at night. I composed new lyrics in my head. It was blissful. I was supremely happy. The Shelter became my refuge, somewhere I could safely ignore the outside world.

I spent that afternoon busking on the South Bank singing some nostalgic songs to the delight of the older folk who passed by and money dribbled into my guitar case. The songs had given me a melancholy journey back into the past with my parents and grandparents. They enjoyed their sing-songs around the piano at family gatherings.

On my way home that evening I fast-forwarded to the twenty-first century. A group of wealthy revellers spilled out of the Savoy hotel. Suddenly I saw something glinting under the street light. It was the gold rim of a wallet.

"Excuse me," I said to a gentleman standing by.

"I think this is yours."

"I do believe it is," he said taking it quickly from my hand as he climbed into his chauffeured limousine.

I watched the car lights disappear. I'm not even a member of the human race. When a dog retrieves something he gets a pat on the head or a biscuit. I am lower than the animal kingdom.

Chapter 8

I held the pebble in the palm of my hand and traced the writing which was etched neatly in purple and felt the little white dove embossed in the top corner. This was the only thing I had left in the world, sad memories of my last moments with Helen. But now I could feel Helen's presence in my life, telling me to move on, to make the most of what I had left. Living on the margins of society, I had begun to realise that a new life could have been waiting for me to reach out to it. I had been almost there and had tried to hoist myself out of the homelessness and helplessness, but it was not that easy to clamber out when the pit was so deep. I was scared of descending even deeper into my misery. Monday mornings were particularly depressing for me and my only comfort was an escape back into my music and books.

One night on my way back into the cardboard, this tiny stretch of side street, I saw a pretty girl, wandering by the river, tall and slender with dark brown eyes, olive skin and long black hair falling over her shoulders. I bent down and extended my hand but the girl shrank away.

"Go away. Leave me alone."

So many homeless people slept around but most of them wanted to keep themselves to themselves. I knew this girl needed help and made another attempt.

"Can I help you?" I asked. But there was terror in her eyes. She had a way of turning her head slightly and looking over her shoulder.

"Get off," she retaliated with a devastating force and a wild frenzy.

We regarded each other without speaking for a moment.

"It's alright I am not going to harm you." I offered her a seat on an old orange box.

She sat with her arms wrapped tightly around her knees and began to fold in on herself. Some of the anger had dissipated but her silence seemed to draw into eternity.

I knew she was hiding from someone, terrified of being seen, still sitting with her face hidden in her arms. She seemed a girl of Eastern European origin, childlike yet already world-weary. Everyone was hiding from someone or something in this place but although I offered to help I didn't really want to get too involved.

I was wrapped up in my own jumble of thoughts but Jock came to the rescue, tumbling down beside the girl, a little more sober than usual.

"Hello little one. What's your name?" Jock reached down into a deep pocket of his filthy coat and offered her a can of Coke, which she snatched from his hand.

"I don't remember. I forget everything. I fall on the steps and bang my head and now I forget everything."

He took out a pencil and an old cigarette packet and I was amazed to see Jock sitting with the girl playing noughts and crosses on the back of the packet. There was an immediate rapport between them. He was chatting easily with the girl as they filled in the noughts and crosses on the battered cigarette box. There was Jock, dressed in a tattered old coat and reeking of stale urine and alcohol, showing some strange new paternal instinct I would never have expected from him.

I listened to snatches of conversation in the dim light.

"I used to have a daughter like you, young and beautiful.... long black hair like yours," he sat staring into nothingness. The girl smoothed her hair with a trembling hand.

"And a beautiful wife too, Caroline was her name. She was the most wonderful wife in the world." Jock stroked the gold ring on his finger. "But I lost both of them. And now here I am a useless old sod."

"You are a very kind man."

"What happened to your wife and daughter?"

"The Notting Hill riots. Well to be honest, it was long after the riots but trouble flared up again. I was in the Navy at the time. There were riots on the streets and houses set on fire. That was how they died, in a house fire. There was nothing anyone could do to save them. But that was a long time ago. And here I am. Took to drink when I heard I had lost everything, my house and family."

"People said, "Why don't you get compensation?" But they didn't know what they were talking about. How would compensation ever bring back my wife and child?"

"Oh you poor man!"

"My daughter was beautiful like you," he said again. "Would you like to come down to the off-licence?"

"No, no!" the scared look returned, but behind those frightened eyes, there was a kind, perceptive young girl, maybe not more than sixteen years old. She would be truly vulnerable here on the streets and needed more protection.

The next morning Jock reached out towards her. "If you come with me to the Shelter, I can get you some food and medical help," but the girl got into a state of hysteria.

"I will jump off that bridge into the river." She was totally disorientated and attacked Jock with high-pitched screams. This had been a simple gesture of help but then I realised that there were psychological problems.

'It's alright", Jock said, "It's just a matter of time. You will be alright in a few days. "You stay here and I will bring you some food and drink."

She looked quizzically at Jock, a fear and mistrust in her eyes. Their lives were all in a mess.

I decided to keep my distance but later I noticed small discrepancies in the girl's lack of memory and had suspicions that she was not all she seemed to be. Irregularities were obvious as a result of several conversations with Jock and something clicked inside my head.

It was another wet Monday morning as I walked down the embankment towards the Shelter. Kate wasn't there and Maura was working in her office. I just intended to have a quick breakfast and a hot drink but Len beckoned me over to his table. He had been reading the papers again and was anxious to have an audience. He was a small bearded man with grey curly hair, aristocratic hair! And he looked like a professor with the small steel-rimmed glasses perched on the end of his nose.

"He shouldn't be here," was one of my fist thoughts. "He is an educated man. An intellectual," but who was I to question?

He was off on his soap box again. "These politicians forget about the state of society. Rather than facing it, dealing with it and trying to speak out for what really matters, justice, humanity, redemption, civil rights, understanding people, making the world a happy place for everyone, giving people a fair go, especially the mentally ill. Mentally illness is too complicated a phenomenon for the medical profession to fully understand. It will always be difficult to quantify how well things are going for any particular individual." His sentences ran into each other without a break.

Sr. Gabriel came over at regular intervals with hot drinks and a plate of cakes.

"The 21st century. I ask you?" Len went on. "Britain is a mucky place, a place adrift on a tide of moral injustices, a place that some of us don't recognise any longer. It is impossible to resist this tide of uncertainty or to make ethical decisions. The government need to behave with responsibility in this global world."

"There is no answer to the important problems in the world. We have to end the exploitation of poor people in the sweat shops, slow down the nuclear arms race, stop terrorism and world hunger. Ensure a strong national defence, prevent the spread of aids, sort out the toxic waste and pollution, improve education, strengthen laws to crack down on crime and illegal drugs. Improve Social Security for senior citizens and conserve natural resources. Economically the country's in a mess. We have to find a way to hold down the inflation rates and we need to lead the way in new technology. Stop people abusing the welfare system. I have got a whole thesis on the subject. I can explain it to you if you have got the time.

I sat facing him in total silence for a long time before answering. "Thanks Len. I will come back and we can discuss some of these issues. I would like to read your thesis, but I must be off now to do a bit of busking, earn a few coppers."

That night I was just dozing off to sleep when I heard the girl on the phone. "Hi Sara, It's me Monika. I escaped from that horrible man. When I left Lithuania I thought I was coming to England for a holiday but I was forced to work every day. Vladimir called himself 'The Godfather' and took control of my life. I was too frightened to complain.... a friend helped me escape. But what good has it done? I am far from home and I have no money and no passport. No one can help me.... No, no. I can't come to see you. Someone watching every minute."

I had heard the conversation and began to sense the significance of her fear and reasons for the mistrust. But I still had problems of my own. My head was in a swirl, everything a mess. Now I realised it wasn't just myself, the entire population of London's homeless was in a similar predicament.

Jock whispered, "Monika, are you still awake? Listen, don't get angry little one. I heard you talk with your friend. You are safe with me. We won't let that nasty man get you. Just tell me how I can help."

"You can't help. If you tell anyone, I am dead. Do you understand?"

"Yes I understand very well. I have met cruel people like him. But you need help. Just lie low for a couple of days and we will work something out. Trust me."

She went absolutely berserk and was clearly out of control again but Jock managed to get her back on an even keel.

As the clock struck midnight I was becoming more and more anxious, about myself and Jock and the girl. Here was a girl in real danger and I was powerless to help. The whole world was in a mess. I felt too restless to sleep, but had just begun to doze off when I heard the muffled ring tone of a mobile phone.

Monika's voice whispered, "Thanks for ringing back. I'm scared Sara. I'm here with some street people. I pretend to have lost my memory but I think they are suspicious. I really need a safer place. But I know he will find me in the end. I would kill myself, not go back to be his slave. He told me lies to get me to London. Promised a nice house and a good job in a bar."

There was a long pause. "You know what it is like. He used me.... those horrible men! No. I can't do that. He has threatened my family if I report him. Yes, I know but he is working with a gang. Even if he locked up I will never be safe. I couldn't go back to Lithuania. He took my passport. I told him I want to go home. He said I must work here for months. I have to pay a lot of money for the journey.... Shh. I have to go. I think there is someone coming.... don't forget to phone me." In between sobs, the girl said something in a foreign language that sounded Eastern European. It was obvious she'd had a bad experience. There was fear in her eyes. The girl was terrified. Each person in this crazy world had their own horror story.

Chapter 9

We had survived another day. Jock brought food and drink for Monika. The sun was shining through the bushes in front of the cardboard and Monika sat down to eat her breakfast.

"Did you ever hear of Churchill," Jock asked, striking up a conversation and trying to distract Monika from her own problems. "Sir Winston Churchill?"

"Yes I think I hear the name."

"It was bitterly cold, the day of Churchill's funeral; huge limousines were driving through the city. We were standing there in the freezing cold waiting, waiting. We queued for hours to view his body, lying in state. But the most moving moment after the funeral service was when they took his body to Oxford by barge. Everyone swarmed down to the river to watch."

"This place reminds me of him and all the things that happened back then. His funeral was in January 1965, the funeral of the Great Sir Winston Churchill. I remember it well. We stood further up the river, me and Caroline. I had baby Emily in my arms, the most beautiful baby in the world. I was home from the Navy on leave. We watched it all with thousands of other people."

Monika listened with sadness in her eyes.

"He had a full state funeral, you know, the only commoner of the twentieth century to have had such an honour. I will never live to see a greater man. Everyone was crying. This is the man who saved our country. It is because of him that we are a free nation."

"And the most amazing thing happened, and I will remember it all my life, the cranes on the dockhands bowed before him, cargo cranes on the River Thames dipping in a last farewell to this great man as the barge bearing his body passed by. The great Sir Winston Churchill's body was carried up the Thames on the Royal Barge on his last journey."

"That is a lovely story," Monika looked up into his eyes in amazement.

I learned more about Jock from these chats with Monika than I could have learned in months, more than anyone in the Shelter knew about him.

It was so obvious that Monika had been forced to work in a brothel as a virtual slave. She would have to die. There was no way they could afford to let the secret of the operation get out and have the police sniffing around. Maybe it happened far more than I realised. After all, I had led a sheltered, middle-class life. I knew nothing of the grim lives of the thousands of young foreign women in the country; many of them were probably disappearing every day with no one to notice their absence. The girls tended to be young and they were usually too scared and confused even to think of escape. Monika was obviously connected to some kind of criminal activity, and whoever was searching for her would soon find her.

Chapter 10

In was the week for new arrivals. Only two days after Monika walked into our lives and just as I was about to settle down for the night, my eye caught sight of a young Asian man who sauntered into our small group. He was handsome with regular features and short jet-black hair.

"Can I get you anything?" I reached out towards him but he glared at me with contempt.

'F*** off. You're just like the rest of them. I don't want any charity from you or anyone else."

The young man moved over to where Monika was sitting and started on his heart-rending life story. Monika was only too keen to listen as it took all the focus away from herself. She reached into her small rucksack to find a bottle of water and the remains of her own sandwich from breakfast which Jock had brought back from the Shelter.

'Here you need something to eat,' she said kindly.

As the conversation struck up between them, I kept my head in a book but I couldn't concentrate. I needed to know more about both of them in order to understand what they were doing here.

They sat up to have a whispered conversation. "I'm Mahmud by the way," he shook her hand. "My parents threw me out and that was what made me so depressed to begin with. I was worried about what was going to happen."

"Just like me. A group further down the river threw me out three days ago and that was when I came here," Monika said.

Mahmud went on. "I had an overbearing father and I struggled for most of my life to try to live up to his expectations. Home was a hostile place. I just had to get out and I moved away to live with my grandparents and finally I dropped out of school."

"One night I climbed out the bedroom window in a fit of anger to avoid a thrashing from my grandfather and never went back. He was as bad as my Dad. My upbringing had completely unhinged me so I had no choice but to make a run for it."

"I cleared out with my grandmother's savings," he laughed, "and by the time the sun had set that evening, here I was on the streets of London. They were always humiliating me. I don't trust adults and I'm determined to make his own way in life. My squabbling parents had sent me off the rails. It was when their aggression towards me became unbearable that I turned to drugs. Their constant fighting and screaming started to affect my school work. They never stopped criticising me and day after day I was confronted with more criticism and conflict and physical abuse from my violent father.

He told me I was a useless layabout and I began to believe him. I suppose you could say I met the wrong crowd but they were young people my own age and they understood me. I want nothing to do with grownups and I hope that jerk over there hasn't been bothering you," he pointed over in my direction.

I heard more whispering and some muffled laughter. "Be on your guard at all times. Keep your mouth shut and your eyes wide open," I warned myself as I watched them out of the corner of my eye. Mahmud had a killing instinct and could probably knock me out in one punch.

At this point I became uneasy. Mahmud could bring Monika down. He could be manipulative particularly with someone as vulnerable as she was. The world had been a very untrustworthy one for Mahmud and he responded in the only language he knew. I knew he could be violent, and dangerous and possibly destructive. There was a sense of revenge in his eyes and in his own admission he was drinking too much and dabbling in drugs, his adolescence now teetering on delinquency. He was a loser, a homeless junkie, and he would take Monika down with him.

Mahmud's aggression brought back some painful memories of my own brother Martin. I dredged up the memories of my unhappy childhood and my concerns for Martin. He had lots of friends but lots of enemies too so he could have been murdered and his body dumped somewhere. Some bodies are never found, swallowed up by concrete in building foundations or motorway extensions. I shuddered at the thought. I could still see the twisted grin on his face. Martin was always stressing me out and could make me angrier than anyone else in the world. He was ruining my life if I let him, with all his aggressive behaviour and constant moaning.

"You are a nerd, wasting your time reading books," Martin used to snatch the book from my hand and I still remembered being in trouble at school when Martin threw one of my text books into the river at the back of the house. I couldn't wait to be older and do things my own way.

To begin with Martin let our Dad boss him about, pretending to be the model son but father soon saw through the facade and one day flew into a rage.

"You are well protected and well respected. Girls love you too. What is your problem? I've had it up to here with your bad moods Martin. You are well fed, have all your faculties, live in the lap of luxury and have at least half a brain. But I intend booking anger management sessions for you."

At this Martin flew into a rage, went up to his bedroom, slammed the door almost off its hinges and beat up the bed instead. That was what he always did. I could see the killer in his eyes. He could have murdered our father on the spot. That was the day of his disappearance.

"Your dinner's getting cold," mother called up the stairs but there was no response. When she went up to his bedroom, she discovered most of his belongings scattered across the floor and some of his favourite things had gone.

But I was back in the present.

Every time Mahmud went off on his rambles to wherever he got his kicks, I tried to develop Monika's trust in order to keep her from falling deeper into misfortune. I offered to buy her water and cigarettes.

"Listen," I said, "I know all about it. I have read a lot in the papers about London's sex slaves. Thousands of women and young girls are working in brothels, saunas and massage parlours in London. Many of them were smuggled into the country from

Eastern Europe and Asia as sex slaves. They are working in a vulnerable position and being exploited by violent and abusive pimps and traffickers. I know they are frequently forced to live in terrible conditions, even sleeping on floors, and are then farmed out and moved around the capital."

"That is what Vladimir did, smuggled me from my own country and put me with those horrible men. Thanks Mr. Kevin, I know you are trying to help me. I need to get money for my phone and I don't know how to charge it."

That was the first time she had used my name. I had made a little breakthrough but I was still worried about what Mahmud would do.

"Give me your phone," I reached over and she willingly handed it to me. "I will charge it and top it up. I have enough money."

"You are a kind man, Mr. Kevin."

As I walked towards the newsagent's I was convinced I saw that mysterious figure in the faded yellow sweatshirt and stone-washed jeans with a baseball cap pulled down over his eyes.

"Calm down!" I told myself. I was allowing my imagination to play games with me again.

Chapter 11

The honking of car horns and rumbling of trains announced another day. It was a foggy beginning to another new day on the streets that made me feel lethargic and I knew I needed to do something about it. My morning routine included my run down the south bank, running, running, fast and furious but going nowhere. I had yet to work out how I would spend my time today, not just today but for the rest of my life. The city had already come to life. My dad had always tried to train me to have a disciplined mind.

"Time for homework, time for play, time for rest." He had always stressed the importance of sufficient hours sleep if one is to perform well at school or in the workplace. It wasn't surprising therefore that I was already devising a rough schedule in my head. I needed a daily routine, to make a bid for a new beginning. I had decided on one particular Sunday afternoon to come alive again, to energise myself. I could see the way my life was gathering speed. My running had restored me into the physical world and did a lot for my self-confidence. It also helped control my aggression which had been a problem since I had developed a guilt complex. In some ways I felt less of an outcast. My music was also an outlet for my frustrations and aggression. Even though there were slim pickings, I opened up my guitar case, took off my jacket and got ready to tune up. I played pretty much the same stuff over and over, the songs I knew people liked.

When I returned to the cardboard, I glanced across at Monika. She was drifting back to sleep again.

"I always feel safer in the daytime," I had heard her tell Mahmud. "The night scares me. That is when they will come to get me."

I watched Monika with a certain amount of uneasiness. There were so many inconsistencies. She was murmuring in her sleep, so vulnerable and so fragile.

Later at the Shelter I met Maura and she took him into her small office. I had told her a little about Monika's plight.

"I have been asking one of our doctors about amnesia and apparently it is often transient, related to some degree of injury or long-term repressed memory, or even a result of psychological or emotional trauma. There is often inability to recall some or all of one's past and either the loss of one's identity or total memory loss. It seems as though Monika may have experienced a traumatic event. Psychological trauma to the brain can be caused, by a blow on the head. Those who suffer from amnesia do not tend to forget their childhood or who they are but have trouble remembering day-to-day events."

"Thanks Maura but since we last talked I have come to the conclusion that Monika is faking her condition. I know there are different kinds of amnesia, which is why I don't want to make judgements and jump to conclusions too quickly. But now I'm not so sure if that's what it is."

"But anyway it's good to know about these things. Many of those people in the streets have experienced some sort of trauma and this can cause amnesia, which is usually temporary and can be triggered by both psychological and physical trauma and as I said, it can be caused by something like a road accident or a blow on the head."

"But how are you yourself?" Maura asked. "I have been thinking about you and I know you will pull through. There is an old Japanese proverb which states that failure is not falling down but refusing to get up. Remember we all need other people; we need to enlist the help of those around us. None of us can afford to be too independent. Although you have to do it by yourself, you can't do it alone. And you must stop blaming yourself."

"I keep telling myself all these things," I said as I let Maura's comforting words sink in. She was already doing so much to lift me out of my depression and get my life back on track.

"I had everything," I told her, "A good home, wealthy parents, a good education and good job and then Helen. She was so vibrant, so alive. But then one day it all fell apart." I could hear the agitation in my own voice. The desperation!

"Life makes no promises," Maura stroked my hand and I blinked back the tears.

I could feel her depth of humanity reaching out to my soul. She encouraged me to talk and be more open about my own condition. I told her how it felt to be suicidal, the feeling of having nothing to live for, how I had held down a good job and then nothing. She had a special way with the homeless. She understood us and empathised with us. Maura asked the questions with such sensitivity. She didn't want to probe but she wanted to get to know me so that she could help.

Opening up and explaining my thoughts and behaviour acted as a form of therapy. I was a pitiful wretch whose heart had been broken but I began to rely on Maura for spiritual and philosophical support which would enable me to come to terms with my situation. After a period of indecision, there was a defining moment when all I understood was that I had to try to rise up, to get free, to resume my road. I crawled out of my hiding place with new hope and ambition. My life began to alternate between order and chaos. I needed to embrace something, something new that would make me feel alert and fearless.

"If you could turn back the clock you would. But why live in guilt?" Maura said. "If you act like something is impossible, it will be. You've got to believe it's possible." A lump swelled up in my throat. Maura was a woman of the greatest compassion and wisdom.

I felt the tension of weeks and months, easing a little and let out a deep breath. "Thank you for coming to get me," I said. She shook her head and smiled across at me.

"That's what I'm here for. Perhaps it is about finally getting closure. Kate tells me that you are one of the most intelligent people she has met. She knows you shouldn't be in a place like this. But I understand. I have met all sorts, believe me. They are not all alcoholics or drug addicts."

My heart missed a beat. Up till that moment, I didn't think Kate knew of my existence. I was just one helpless being in a long line queuing up for something to eat. I could see the wisdom of

Maura's words." Life isn't fair but it's still good. When in doubt, just take the next small step." She had helped me keep my feet firmly on the ground.

"Now off to your breakfast," Maura laid a kindly hand on my shoulder. "And please feel free to come along to my office anytime you would like to have a chat." On the way out she led me over to the storeroom and gave me another warm jumper.

"How am I ever going to thank you for all this?" I said.

"It's not from me," she said. "There are lots of kind people out there who don't want you to freeze on the streets. And remember one day you will know the future and you will see everything clearly. Be patient."

She was enabling me with self-analysis. I couldn't fulfil my goals, ambitions and dreams without her. My life was much richer for having her on my side. She was helping me with a second chance, an opportunity to get back on track, humanising me after I'd been dehumanised. In some ways it was giving me back my identity. I was becoming a person again, changing my attitudes to others as well. It was about my day-to-day survival. Maura dramatically changed all that. She had proven to be such a positive life-changing force in my life although there were still plenty of reminders of the past and of how far I had still got to travel but in the meantime Maura was my safety-line.

I was at a big crossroads and I had an opportunity to put the past behind me. For the first time, I felt like I was almost ready for it.

I could see the wisdom in her words, "Life isn't fair but it's still good. When in doubt, just take the next small step."

In the dining room Kate was already rushing around seeing to everyone's needs. She was strikingly beautiful but in a simplistic way, no make-up and no pretences although still a bit shy. As I arrived we looked at each other and although we lived in different worlds I could feel a definite pull between us. Or maybe it was just my imagination or wishful thinking.

"Good morning! How are you today," I ventured to ask.

"Good morning Kevin. I'm fine and how are you?" Unlike the others, she always took the trouble to stop and hear the reply.

"Fine thanks. This is a warm place in a cold world." I was still self-conscious but there was so much I wanted to tell her. I wanted to pour out my heart and I knew she would be a good listener. I wanted to tell her everything I was feeling but the words just drifted away. "She doesn't want to hear a sob story from a useless, good-for-nothing, shirker like me. I just need to get my life together and forget the self-pity," I thought.

Then it happened. She turned back and looked right at me. Her gaze lingered for a moment as I looked into her eyes. She waited a split second and smiled at me. Not another word, just a smile. A warmth between us. That smile held more meaning than any words could have. I saw honest and undisguised tenderness that completely disarmed me. I was stunned and speechless. I felt dazed yet strangely calm. I was convinced that I had experienced something that had changed my life. As she turned away I could see the serious reflective expression on her face as she listened to someone else's problems. She had an ease and a bearing that I had never seen in anyone before. It was at once arresting and modest, a kind of natural, inborn grace.

"Take it easy," I told myself. "I am being an idiot. We are worlds apart." I moved across and took my chair at the furthest corner of the room.

Just then, through the small window, I could see Jock descending the stairs gingerly with his thin hand that trembled slightly and held onto the rails in a helpless way, sometimes falling and missing the steps but I knew it wasn't just from the booze. He groped his way down the metal stairs, hanging on the handrail and feeling with his foot for each step. Everything about him was undernourished. He was going downhill steadily and it could be seen in his frail body as he stood at the counter, shoulders hunched as though he had no right to be there and often refusing things which he desperately wanted and needed.

"I have tied Tatters outside onto the railing," he whispered in my ear. Jock's little dog went everywhere with him. He had followed Jock home one night and had stayed at his heels ever since. "Tatters! What better name for a wee homeless dog? "Jock said and the name had stuck.

He came over to my table and said, "I want you to get the wee laddie a mouthful of something to eat, and don't forget food and drink for Monika." I was aware that Jock was finding it increasingly difficult to carry things so I promised to get supplies for all of us.

On stepping out of the Shelter, I was blinded by a flash of lightening, my mind transported back to my father's funeral. My mother stood behind me as the cemetery was lit up. As we consoled each other, loud rumbles of thunder and lightning flashed once more with thick, black clouds and rooks scattering this way and that in their confusion. In my own confusion I saw a strong healthy man relying on the charity of strangers, depending on senior citizens or on hand-outs from young people like Kate catering for my every need.

She would probably think I was ridiculous, a disgrace to humanity. Was I out of my mind, choosing the easy option and dropping out of society? I had created my own misery and it was too painful to think about. Did Kate think I was unlucky or did she think that I was a victim of my own selfishness? "What is a beautiful young girl doing in a place like this?"

That evening I played some sad music and watched all the people rushing home. A storm was creeping over the city as I packed my guitar and headed back towards the cardboard.

The lightning flashed across the river lighting up a watchful presence, the strange dark figure on the bridge, a black baseball cap covering his face.

Chapter 12

One morning back in the Shelter, Len finished his breakfast, stood up and said to anyone who might be interested in listening, "You won't be seeing me again. I'm not spending another winter on the streets. It's time I had a comfortable bed and a warm house at my age. I'm off to North Yorkshire to live with my daughter. She has been asking me for ages. I couldn't stand another winter in this place."

"But hasn't she got three young children? You don't like modern kids," I said.

"Yes, but this is different. They are family, my own flesh and blood and I don't want to miss my grandchildren growing up. We speak every Sunday on the phone and last week I suddenly became aware of all I was missing in my own family."

Len had all his belongings in a large black sack outside the Shelter.

"Well that's it. Good luck mate," I gave him a pat on the back.

Old Len had been our constant source of information and put the world to rights each morning. He would be missed.

He walked towards the door and gave a brief wave over his shoulder.

"But who's going to keep us up to date with the daily news," someone shouted across the room.

"That's your problem. I'm off. They have been asking me for ages, and I want to see my grandchildren

"Are you OK for the train fare," Maura asked as he went into the corridor.

Of course I am. I've never taken charity from any one."

There must be an irony there somewhere I thought. I had seen Len sitting out even in the bitter cold with a placard that read. *'Spare a copper for a hungry old man.'* He obviously got all his food at the Shelter so I reckoned he had a nice little hoard of money stashed away somewhere.

"I'm off up there where the air is clear. Beautiful blue skies and magnificent scenery, away from all this mess and pollution."

"Good Luck," Maura said.

Outside the Shelter door he picked up all his belongings in the black sack and shuffled his way towards a bus to take him to the station.

There was a sadness in the air and I was in a melancholy mood. The heavy overnight storms and freak downpours gave way to bright sunshine over the river. I had stopped trembling and needed to do something constructive.

I walked to Richard's flat to get my guitar, always careful with my timing. Richard had already gone to work. There was no need to keep reminding him of my dire situation.

"The best music comes from a broken heart." I had heard someone say this back in my college days. Tragic events can change a performer's music and the arts helped connect with the world. Sorrow had always affected creative expressions.

Today I thought of Edith Piaf and her tragic life, with her poignant ballads and heart-breaking voice. As I walked across the bridge, I hummed an old favourite of my mother's. '*Non, je ne regrette rien*', which was played at my father's funeral. Some time ago my mother had shown me a video of Piaf's funeral through the streets of Paris following her early death from liver cancer.

"Piaf was a street child too," I thought and now her life story was more relevant to my own life.

I thought of the video and how Piaf's sad and valiant life story stole the hearts of many as thousands followed her funeral procession, which was the only time, since the end of World War Two that Parisian traffic came to a complete standstill as '*Non, je ne regrette rien*' sounded out all over the city. When I reached my busking spot, I tuned up my guitar and played it now in my own humble way.

Later I struck up a Harry Nilsson song, *Everybody's talking at me. I don't hear a word they're saying, only the echoes of my mind.*

People stopping staring, I can't see their faces, only the shadows of their eyes...

A few coins dribbled into the guitar case. Then I tried a Billie Holiday number, my own rendition of Blue Moon. But I knew that nobody could really do justice to her songs. I wished I had her amazing ability to breathe life into a song. Like me, Billie had struggled with life. She sang about anti-racism and discrimination and wanted to stand up for equal rights. Although she was considered by many to be the greatest jazz vocalist of all time, she died penniless.

But my problems pale into insignificance when I thought of Piaf and Billie Holiday.

There he was again that strange person in the faded yellow sweatshirt standing at the side of a pillar as I sang. I glanced up quickly again but there was no one there. My imagination playing havoc with my brain.

"Calm down," I told myself as I stood there were tears in my eyes, thinking of my own fears and all these sad people and all the sadness throughout the world. At the end of my session, I packed up my guitar and quickly returned to Richard's flat. I left a hasty note on the phone pad, "Thanks mate!" I felt it was important that Richard was always aware of my visits. Sometimes he left little friendly messages for me.

That night the moon came out again with new hope, but Monika sat there cold, shivering with teeth chattering.

"Here, little one," Jock with trembling hands spread an old blanket across her knees. The warm day had turned into a long, cold night. It was difficult to sleep with the freezing cold and the noise of the traffic screeching to a standstill at the traffic lights, and the trains thundering out of Charring Cross station. The next morning I got Monika some things she needed, a phone top-up, some cigarettes, food and drink.

The following night I came home after sauntering along the river. It was another cold night and a white haze lay over the river. Everyone seemed to have settled for the night. Jock was already snoring and Monika was in one of her restless sleeps. I read for a while by the street light and the clock struck twelve. Just then I thought I heard a noise in the bushes. I waited in the darkness. A strong breeze was blowing up so I told myself it was just a gust of wind. But my imagination was getting the better of me.

Suddenly I was struck on the back of the head with a heavy object. The blow was repeated and I remembered coming round some time later. I wasn't sure how long I had been unconscious. Overcome with confused feelings, I saw the river in the distance. If only I could get to the river. It would be cooler and brighter with the street lights. I was scared of the darkness. For the first time I felt real fear. It could have been my life. I was now fully aware of the dangers living on the streets. My whole body was feeling weak and I couldn't move my head. Then I heard footsteps coming towards me. This time I was on the alert but it was only Mahmud. He walked right past me in a dazed stupor.

My head was throbbing with pain. When I could move again, I sat up, hunching over in an effort to ease the pain. I looked around but couldn't see anyone, only Mahmud rummaging through some dirty old bag, looking for a fix no doubt.

I must have dozed off but was suddenly awakened by sunrise, huge streaks of light radiating outward in all directions. Tentatively, I shifted my body, checking my limbs. "The fall!" I remembered. I ached all over from the fall but only my head showed any signs of malfunction. I looked around in shocked horror. Monika was gone!

Walking over towards her makeshift bed I picked up her frayed sleeping bag and spotted her mobile phone lying beneath the rubble. Suddenly I had the most dreadful fear for the safety of all these young girls and I feared for the older folk too, the elderly are easily bullied, often neglected or patronised, forgotten, deprived of basic care, even abused. But what could I do?

And even though it was broad daylight, still the watchful figure stood on the bridge, a strange glint in his eyes.

Chapter 13

By late morning, I had regained my equilibrium and spent the entire day searching for Monika. Jock was distraught and had done his bit in the search in his own frail way. In the evening, I walked along the river and the sight of the sun was forming a cross on St. Paul's Cathedral. It was evening again and the sun was blood red and sinking rapidly. Then all the domes, spires, turrets and pinnacles of London rose in inky blackness like the darkness of my soul. Two limousines were ferrying the last party-goers to their luxurious homes. I was travelling along life's highways in a broken down truck, the dim headlights flickering and failing. I stood shivering on the path. Jock and I were still shocked and despairing over Monika's disappearance.

That evening I found Sara's number on Monika's phone. I wasted no time in phoning the number but didn't want to give her the news over the phone. I suggested it was best if she came over to see me. Later that evening a twig snapped a few yards away and I froze. My nerves on edge, I forced myself to calm down, hold my breath and stay still. But then Sara stepped out of the shadows. I told her quickly about Monika's disappearance and watched her horrified reaction. Although her voice sounded normal, there were tears running down her face. Then it struck me that she might also be in some danger.

"We are all doing our best to find her, but it seems to be an impossible task," I said. "Go back home and stay there until you have heard further news from me. There's really not much you can do in a city this size.

But it was just another day in Mahmud's life, caught up in the drugs menace which was blighting modern society. He was becoming gaunt and painfully thin and often seen with an older man thought to be a dealer, revealing the bleak truth of how addicts are unable to hide their habit.

Len used to say, "The Government should be doing more to tackle the problem. They are just not doing enough. People are seen taking drugs in the open on a daily basis, in broad daylight. One regularly finds needles and drugs paraphernalia in doorways and alleyways. This life is hell. The use of crack cocaine is rocketing. Latest figures show the number of crack users caught by police has risen in the past ten years."

The price of drugs had plummeted but Mahmud still had to scrounge around, stealing for whatever money he could lay his hands on. He was now battling with depression and had even considered suicide. He had taken a tumble once again and had become volatile and helpless. Although he was a drug addict, I didn't exactly know what kind. Perhaps heroin. All I had seen him do was coke. He seemed to be on methadone now but had done other drugs.

I was careful around drugs and didn't consider them as an escape out of my misery. I had seen what they've done to others over the years. I didn't like talking with Mahmud when he was high. There had been raids, arrests and interrogations. Mahmud was frustrated by policemen on the streets, the frisking, the nights in police cells, the way he had to keep walking, constantly dodging the next arrest. His world was shifty, painful, and menacing. This was all part of his general delinquency and the drink and drugs were steadily driving him to self-destruct. I knew that he was deep into alcoholism and consuming vast quantities of vodka and cocaine. He quickly became addicted to the hallucinatory drugs and was arrested and fined for the possession of cannabis. His life was a haunted, terrifying nightmare. He looked blankly when he heard of Monika's disappearance.

All this was dragging me down. I had reached new levels of despair, my recovery dissolving before my eyes. I now faced the hell of having to live with imaginary ghosts from the past, an unresolved future stretching before me, the present a blur. The future was now out of focus and the past was a dark shadow. I was frozen in one speck of time, taking each day as it came surviving by my wits. I was estranged from my family and desperate to escape my past, alone but preferred it that way. No stranger would ever understand why my life had taken this unexpected turn. People are afraid of being abandoned or scared to pursue their most important dreams feeling unable to achieve them and consequently turn to the bottle. But I knew from Jock's experience that the bottle doesn't make people happy. It doesn't solve anything. I wondered if my brother Martin was still alive or if he had taken to drugs.

Conditions got significantly worse but I was determined to cling to my daily routines but now my running was a constant search for Monika. The one fixed point in my week which I looked forward to was my Saturday and Sunday mornings at the Shelter. Daily routines consisted of my morning run each time taking a different direction and searching all the homeless sites in the area. Routines had been ingrained into my mind. My life couldn't function without them. I had breakfast and lunch at the shelter, but until Monika was found my reading and busking were now on hold.

But Kevin was unaware of the mysterious being standing in the shadows.

Chapter 14

It was only seven a.m. but the school was already buzzing with excitement and frayed nerves all over the place, everyone fussing over display boards, last-minute photocopying and lesson plans.

The day of the dreaded OFSTED inspection had arrived but everyone was so well-prepared and Pauline, the new Head, had been reassuring. She constantly reminded them, "You are the experts in your field. Some of these inspectors have come from secondary schools and have never stood before a class of young children. They are experts in one subject but you are experts in ten or twelve. They can do nothing but admire you in the way you deliver the curriculum. Just stay calm. I know we have no problems and we are quite ready to let them see our worth."

Pauline had done an amazing job in turning the place around. The school had been labelled 'special measures'. There had been no account taken of the excellent pastoral care that had been offered to pupils and the additional support for children with special educational needs.

But Pauline was aware that the inspectors had been right. There had been a serious drop in academic standards and they owed it to the children to give them the best all-round education possible. She had provided extra in-service training and brought in advisors from the Local Education Authorities in every subject area. Staff morale was now at an all-time-high. She was right. They had the expertise and confidence to carry it through.

Kate waved to Beki her colleague next door. She tried to put a brave face on it all. "Good luck Beki and make sure you get thirty sets of little fingers crossed before those inspectors walk in the door."

"Good luck. We'll be fine. There's no need to be nervous Kate. I know it couldn't have come at a worse time for you. But just remember how unruly these little monsters were a couple of months ago and how we have managed to get them into shape."

Kate wasn't so sure. Her nerves were still on edge after all she had been through and she had still got three or four really disruptive children in her class who could wreck any well-planned lesson. The inspectors would be looking for teaching skills, class control and her own confidence amongst other things."

"Chin up!" Beki knew that Kate was apprehensive about the whole procedure. It was her first inspection. She didn't really know what to expect and it had been a particularly bad year for her in lots of ways.

"See you later," Beki said with two sets of fingers crossed.

At the end of the day, after all the inspectors had gone and the last child had left the school building Kate popped her head into Beki's classroom. "Phew! That was something!" she said.

Beki was tidying up, picking pencils and paper off the floor. She had usually read the riot act and made the children tidy up after themselves but today her mood had to be subdued. She had kept her voice calm and gentle.

They sat down together on top of the small tables. Beki's mind was in turmoil and she found it hard to focus on the curriculum targets for the next day but Kate jumped up. "I will go and get some coffees and see if there are any of those cakes left over from our elevenses. I don't really want to go into the staffroom to listen to all their moaning or boasting or the endless post-mortems. Anyway there is something I want to tell you."

When she got back they sat down to relax over their coffee. They did a little bit of collaborative planning, for about ten minutes. They would often work together until after six o'clock and travel home in the dark. "And they say teaching is a cosy little nine to four number, with thirteen weeks holiday," Beki used to say. "And you know our answer to these people, if it's that easy why don't you come and join us. The pay's not bad either compared to what you guys earn up there in the stock market or in your cushy little bank jobs."

"It wasn't so bad after all," Kate said. "Like I guessed, a couple of little horrors tried to disrupt the lessons. But Trish was a brick. You couldn't get a better classroom assistant. Every time trouble raised its head, she was there on the spot, distracting them and moving them on to something which she knew would interest them. I couldn't have coped today without her. And indeed I wouldn't have survived this past year if it hadn't been for Trish."

"I agree you are blessed with Trish's support. Wish I could say the same but I know Christine is doing her best. I believe Trish is working towards her degree and qualified teacher status. She will make a brilliant teacher."

"Maybe we will take them out for a meal, now that it is all over."

"But Pauline is taking us all to her favourite restaurant regardless of the results. It was to be our reward for all the hard work we have put in. She has confidence in us and the parents were with us all the way."

"Oh yes, I had forgotten that, too busy with all the preparation. Well, maybe we will buy some flowers for Trish and Christine. I'll arrange it if you like."

Beki suddenly sat up and looked Kate straight in the eye. "Well what is it? What was it you wanted to tell me? I'm bursting to hear it. But I knew there was something brewing. Your eyes seemed to have a new sparkle and sometimes I watched you sitting there at assembly with a smile on your face, clearly your mind on something else, while the rest of us just sit with our usual haggard faces. You're in love, aren't you?"

"Yes, but I want to tell you in the strictest confidence."

"But surely if you're in love, you want the whole world to know."

Kate hadn't intended telling anyone about her feelings for Kevin. She even tried telling herself it was useless even to think about any future in their relationship especially after the year of hell she had had with Harry. She had sworn she would never look at another man again but here she was falling into the same old trap.

"It's Kevin. I told you about him before. He comes into the Shelter every morning. But please Beki, don't breathe a word to anyone."

"But how do you know you can trust him," Beki asked.

"I just do, instinctively. I don't know how I know. There is just something different about him."

"Hey you're madly in love with him, aren't you? But go easy. You hardly know him. Start to believe in yourself again. Set your sights high. You're a qualified teacher and he's a nobody."

"Don't say that." The tears were welling up in Kate's eyes. "Don't talk about setting my sights high. Harry had his own business, loaded with money, charming in every way or so I thought."

"But now you are going to the other extreme. You can't go from one disastrous relationship to another. Just try to think back. You are still showing the scars physically and mentally. Have you forgotten that final night when he beat you black and blue and you ended up in hospital. Surely you must remember all that. The broken ribs. The insults. The suspicions!"

"But this is different. I am madly in love with Kevin and he loves me too."

Beki threw her arms around her. "Sorry Kate. I just don't want you to get involved in something you may regret later. How do you know he will not turn out like Harry."

"I know why you would want to think that and I know everyone else is going to say the same. That is why I want to keep it quiet for a while. But I was bursting to tell someone and I know I can trust you. Promise me. Not a word."

"Listen Kate, you don't have to ask. You know you can always trust me." She handed Kate some more tissues.

"Thanks Beki. I don't know what I would do without a friend like you."

"But sorry to be the devil's advocate. Even if he didn't batter you around like Harry, how could he ever support you especially if you wanted to have children together? But I know it won't come to that. It will all fizzle out in its own good time. Believe me. It has happened to me before, falling in love with the wrong person. And now I have Michael, good old solid-as-a-rock Michael, working his socks off as an accountant and saving like mad so that we can get married next year. He keeps reminding me that I won't ever have to work again if we start a family."

But Kate interrupted. "I know Beki and I am so pleased for you. Michael is a great guy and I know you will both be very happy.

But I am serious about Kevin. It's not some idle infatuation. It's not going to go away. And I know he is a kind and loving person. Money doesn't mean anything to me anymore."

"What does he look like? A silly question. I guess he looks just like any other homeless junkie."

"He's not a junkie," Beki noticed Kate's anger rising and she decided to go easy on her.

"He's tall, dark and handsome."

Beki rolled her eyes to heaven.

"Lovely grey eyes, very intelligent and very articulate. What more do you want to know? Oh and he's no ordinary street person. He is clean shaven, has a shower every morning and is polite to everyone. Maura thinks the world of him."

"Well, yes, but Maura doesn't want to marry him. How often have you been out together?"

"Well we haven't yet."

"What?" Beki shouted. "You haven't been out together yet? So how do you know he loves you?"

"I just know instinctively. The way he looks at me."

"Listen babe, whatever happens, I am with you all the way. Now cheer up. Go home and forget all about this nasty old inspection."

Kate held Beki's hand. "I would like you to see Kevin. If you go along the South Bank when he is busking you will see what I mean. I will have to stay out of sight. Sometimes I go there on my own and listen to his singing but he doesn't see me."

"You sure have got it badly! But yes. if it pleases you, I'll go but mind you, I think the whole thing is crazy."

Chapter 15

It had been a time of nightmares or hallucination and I tried to snap myself out of it.

On my way down the embankment, a stream of people flowed in and out to the stations. Everything had become a blur of faces and voices. I took a deep breath telling myself to calm down.

When I entered the Shelter, Maura called me into her office. I think she noticed the worry and despair on my face. Maybe she had seen the strain, the tiredness and the effects of my desolation which I had tried to hide from her. She was a woman of the greatest compassion. I could now see her trying to read the turmoil and confusion behind my expression.

"Is everything OK?" she asked.

My voice was thin and hesitant when I told her all about the attack and Monika's disappearance.

"Oh my goodness," she said. "This is dreadful news and such a setback for you."

I thought I had moved on, with a new life waiting around the corner. I was on top of the world. But quite suddenly and unexpectedly my old paranoia had returned.

"The world out there on the streets is a cruel place, without the comfort of a family, a home where you are cherished and loved, which is all a person really needs in this world."

"I thought I had found all of those things."

"Try not to worry too much about Monika. Even if she has been captured and returned to the sex ring, just remember that she escaped before and can do it again."

"A journey of a thousand miles begins with a single step. You can't do it in one night," Maura said. "Believe it or not, the secret is here in the present. If we pay attention to the present, we can improve upon it. And if you improve on the present, what comes later will also be better and I know that is what you are trying to do. The real power lies in the human heart, its courage, its resilience. You have all of that. Things will work out in the end," Maura gave me a reassuring smile, truly feeling for me then.

"It's going to be ok. I promise. You have got what it takes. Slow down. Take one step at a time. Maybe everything is predestined." I felt almost in tears.

Maura took me under her wing. Her voice was tender and she made me feel a glimmer of hope.

She encouraged me to talk again about my own situation and I knew she understood the misfortunes that had come into my fife and pushed me to desperation. She knew that talking about it was therapeutic. She was a great listener. She was one of those people who actually listened to every single word and remained focused on me and only me and didn't talk over me. She genuinely cared about what I was saying. I wanted this so badly, this second chance, this chance at real redemption.

"You wanted to tell me about your brother," she said.

I didn't go into all the details.

"Martin was always watching from the shadows, listening outside doors always trying to catch people out. I tried to stand up to his bullying when it would have been easier to have run indoors and told my patents. He had a sadistic nature and was a monster at times. He flattered the girls. They all loved him but none would stay with him. I made the mistake of tolerating his insidious behaviour. I should have risen up when the brutality became too much to bear. I had tried to stand my ground against his bullying but I had become his punch bag."

"You have suffered a lot. You are a righteous man and there is no need for you to sleep rough on the streets. You deserve better than that. You can move on and have a nice life again. Go now and have some breakfast." Maura had been my guiding light and had encouraged me to talk through my problems rather than keeping them bottled up.

Before going through for my shower and shave, I thanked her, "You have no idea how grateful I am for all the time you have given me, for your support and advice," I said.

"Things will get better. The worst is nearly over now." We sat for another moment in silence. I was trying to forget everything that had happened to me. I was going to have to get out of there if I was to survive, going to save my self-respect.

Sr. Gabriel was the first one to greet me when I reached the dining room, "Ah, there you are Kev. I was beginning to wonder about you. Grab a seat and I will bring everything to you."

"Thank you, Sister," I shook her hand for the first time. "You are an amazing lady."

"Ah go on you and your blarney," we both laughed.

After a hot breakfast, I was beginning to feel a lot calmer. I thanked Sr. Gabriel and waved across to the people behind the counter who had prepared the food.

Before I left that morning Maura came towards me, "Come back into my office for a minute."

I had been stressed out the night before and it was good to unburden on Maura. We talked again about Monika's disappearance and I told her a little about my past, about my guilt and anguish.

"You must try and shake off the guilt. None of this is your fault" she said.

Then she talked about homelessness in general.

"There are all sorts of reasons why people are out there on the streets. You will meet a whole range of different people here and they are all here for different reasons. These reasons can be numerous, such as the breakup of a marriage or relationship, the loss of a job which in turn can lead to the repossession of their home or inability to pay the rent. One of the main causes is an addiction or abuse of drugs. Others become homeless because of a mental illness. And then there is shell shock. People who have served in the armed forces often find it impossible to cope with 'civvy' street when they come out, because of the traumas experienced. Others are running away from an abusive relationship. And there are the young, vulnerable girls like Monika, exploited by the sex trade. Others are escaping violent homes and some with stars in their eyes believing running away will lead to complete happiness."

"The reasons are many and it could happen to anyone. But sadly it is impossible to help all of them. Homeless people come from all walks of life and social background. Some young homeless people will refuse any help that is offered for a number of reason, they may have been abused in care and lost trust in adults or shattered in some other way, lost faith in humanity in general."

I knew that Maura had assessed my own situation.

"You must remember there is always someone to help, someone to talk to if you want to talk," she said. "Each step forward, no matter how small, that is what we are here for, to offer help, support and encouragement in the hope of transforming lives."

"I know that and I am so grateful for all the support I have received from you and all your staff and volunteers." She was trying to take me out of this place of so much anger and grief where I was alone, displaced. She was helping me shake off my feeling of anxiety, depression and guilt which had been a current running through me and feeding into everything I did. It was a vicious circle. We talked endlessly about my situation, how it had started and how I was going to bring it to an end.

I wondered what she really thought about me or if my life could ever really be transformed. People like Kate gave up their free time to help people like myself. They gave freely and generously of their time with no expectations of recompense. There was an immeasurable spirit of giving in this place. A service which would not be delivered without these people. I was in awe of their work.

Maura went on to outline the services offered at the Shelter. "I think you already know about most of the services we have on offer here at the Shelter. As you know, we give primary services such as food, showers, clothes, laundry and medical advice. Did you know that we have art, drama and group skills as well as pastoral support and help with form-filling and debt counselling. There is also a GP clinic, nursing care, specialist mental health workers, specialist drug and alcohol abuse workers, and things like chiropodists and dental examination.

But I had a feeling there was something else on her mind. She had told me most of this before.

"But we have to maintain and respect professional boundaries between ourselves and clients and have respect for client confidentiality. As you can probably guess, we have rules and regulations for our voluntary workers such as trying not to convey inappropriate and misleading signals to clients, never visiting a client in their 'home' or agreeing to meet them outside. Special friendships that are created in this way invariably break up when the volunteer leaves. The client is then left feeling let down and perhaps more vulnerable than before. In the street volunteers may be polite and acknowledge them, but prolonged conversations are not allowed. And they must never take clients home with them or take them for coffee. They are never allowed to give or lend money to clients but are encouraged to refer them to a member of staff who will ensure that they receive the food or assistance that they require. Often their greatest need is to be listened to. Volunteers should not overburden themselves with clients' needs and problems. Exchanging information about clients or each other can so easily develop into gossip."

I had a good idea where all this was leading.

"I have noticed that you have a special eye for Kate, not that you show it in any overt way, but people my age are aware of the signals. And I think she likes you too. It's not that she gives you undue attention. Well, it's just that she seems a different person when you are around and as I said earlier, special friendships that are created in this way invariably break up when the volunteer leaves. You could then be left feeling let down and perhaps more vulnerable than before."

"So this is what it is all about," I thought. She had called me in for this little pep talk. I myself was aware that there was some chemistry between Kate and myself but now I must be determined not to say or do anything that would harm her or jeopardise her position as a voluntary worker.

"She has her own professional career and doesn't need to get into a useless relationship with someone like me," I thought. "She must have lots of admirers."

Before I left, Maura said, "Remember Monika escaped before. She will again."

The next Saturday afternoon Kate had finished her shift in the Shelter. She told me later that she knew where she could find me at this time of the evening and wanted to listen to my music before catching her train home. She stood at a safe distance and listened, but at the end, breaking all the rules in the book, she came over and shook my hand. "That was beautiful," I just stood there awe-struck.

As she turned to walk up to Waterloo station, she saw a young man dressed in a baseball cap and a '*Texas Rangers*' jersey. He went over in her direction. "Hi there, I'm Max. What's a pretty girl like you doing with that waster? You don't want to have anything to do with the likes of him," he said. "Come and I will buy you a coffee." Kate just kept on walking, looking straight ahead, and he followed for some time but knowing he was defeated, he called after her. "Another time maybe."

Chapter 16

"There's nae a better whiskey than Stewarts Cream of the Barley." Jock was muttering to himself. "Aye Wee Laddie don't you think so?" Tatters wagged his tail as Jock patted his head. The little dog had started following him everywhere he went and it became impossible to shake him off. "Tatters," he said, "That's a good name for you. From now on you're my own wee dog, two auld battered beggars, both in tatters." A stooped old man with a lame leg and a little dog limping at his heels. "Two auld cripples, what will become of us?"

During the past month I had watched him stumbling on. The wind howled. His old parka was held tightly around his body flapping in the wind, allowing it to freeze his bones. Jock started shivering, a little trembling at first and then continuously. He had his own priorities, a quiet swig, communing with himself, sometimes wallowing in self-pity and disappointment slipping away into anti-social, delinquent mode. But at other times he was singing and telling jokes, amusing people at the Shelter, endearing himself to everyone. He was a man of many wasted talents, not only with words and images but also music. At the summer party in the Shelter, Jock stood there like a Shakespearean actor delivering a soliloquy. He was a talented, clever, passionate, man but his words were becoming slurred, anaesthetised by alcohol.

On the streets Tatters limped along at his heels or was tucked up beneath Jock's left arm. They navigated their way from the Shelter to the off-licence and back to the cardboard. This was their daily routine. In his previous life, he had a career in the Navy and had been invalided out with just short of twenty years service and no proper pension. It was the trauma of civilian life and the loss of his wife and daughter that drove him to the streets.

Dirty, shabby-looking, homeless and lonely, he sought solace in large swigs of whisky. The waist button of his trousers was replaced by a safety pin and tied with a piece of twine. When he ended up in court it was usually on a charge of disturbing the peace. There were long list of misdemeanours. He had a dark scar on his cheek as a result of a brawl in his navy days and had spent his life going from fight to fight. Nelson's Column had been boarded up for restoration, when they had to clean off the muck that had accumulated over the years. Like Nelson, Jock too had served his time in the Navy but no one was in a hurry to help clean him up.

"You must try to eat to keep up your strength," I constantly told him during the past couple of months.

His memory loss had been caused by alcohol abuse. Sometimes he had severe problems recalling a simple story, going off at tangents, with lists of unrelated words, uncoordinated movements and the loss of feeling in his fingers and toes.

In the off-licence, the sales assistant ignored the smell. "So long as we had money in our pockets we were welcome clients and tolerated." Jock used to say. But that wasn't entirely true. They had built up a good rapport with Jock. They used to have a laugh and a chat together and they always treated him with respect.

The Christmas party at the Shelter was the last time Jock had ventured out on the streets. He held onto my arm with Tatters, rarely straying from his side, now close at our heels hobbling along with his little lame leg. He pricked his drooping ears at some noise by the river's edge, barked a little and ran beside us ready for the day's excitement, his small intelligent face nuzzling against Jock's leg. Then his tail drooped, not ready to wag again. "Terriers are splendid robust little dogs," Jock said. Tatters' thick coat defied the wind and rain, snow and sleet. Old Jock was not so lucky; a grizzled and gnarled little man.

We tethered Tatters to the railings and I helped Jock down the iron steps. "And don't forget Wee Tatters, two old cripples keeping each other company for a while and who knows there might just be some wee scraps of leftovers for him."

In the dull December afternoon, the Shelter provided some respite for all of us, cramped but with a warm atmosphere.

Jock had literally to drag himself now holding onto the rails. Sister Gabriel came over and took his arm to guide him to a seat. "My last Christmas here," Jock said.

"Don't say that Jock. Sure you'll be here for many a long year to come," she helped him into his seat and saw that he had everything he needed.

People jostled between the tables and hot drinks were passed around. A large Christmas tree brightened the room and the place was illuminated with a myriad of coloured fairy lights. After the excellent Christmas dinner, volunteers started to hand round presents from under the Christmas tree.

"Would you like a bottle of something?" Sr. Gabriel asked Jock and a glimmer of a smile came across his face as he pointed to something that looked like a bottle of wine wrapped in glittering Christmas paper.

With his frail hands, he ripped the paper off. "Blimey it's a bottle of bubble bath," he said. "You can have it lad," he handed it to me, "And we will throw you in the river to soak." I laughed and thanked him.

"Much better for you than whiskey," Sr. Gabriel laughed but Jock didn't have the energy to care anymore. At the end of the session Maura slipped him another gift.

"No, I'm OK. There is nothing I need any more," Jock's was wheezing and his voice was almost a whisper.

"Take it easy. You deserve it," Maura said, "for keeping us all entertained over the years" This time he was in luck. A box of chocolates. He gave Maura a glimmer of a smile. After the volunteers had entertained us with their songs and sketches, we hobbled back to the cardboard but from that day Jock never ventured outside on the streets.

I watched dear old Jock lose his grip on life which had been on a downward spiral since Monika's disappearance. He thought of her as his long-lost daughter and she had brought out a new, caring side, bringing out a paternal instinct in his battered old mind. It was a cold March morning with a light scattering of snow and daffodils beginning to open their buds along the verge of the path but the long winter months seemed everlasting and every tree on the embankment was painted silver by the frost.

Jock continued to listen but his mind wandered. I brought back drinks and a little food but he was losing his appetite. He had long since given up the alcohol.

"Are you alright?" I asked.

"I'm done for lad. But I'm not afraid of death. Tonight I will walk the streets of glory, and sit with angels in the realm of the lord with Sandra and my baby and Monika.

"Shh, you're not going anywhere just yet. Let me wrap you up a bit warmer."

I knew how much he had missed Monika and it was after her disappearance that he seemed to have lost his will to live.

"Dying is like shore leave in the navy but the beauty is that it lasts for all eternity," there was a small smile on his face.

He seemed to be waking from a long sleep but his eyes were glazed. He had been living on the margins of society. This was the only life he had known since he had lost his wife and daughter. Jock needed attention. He was in need clean clothes, a good wash but I was fighting a losing battle. I had to go to the Shelter and get him a change of clothes but he was stubborn. It was difficult to get him to change and virtually impossible to get him to have a wash. For the next few weeks I went on with my life, moving around distractedly and keeping a close eye on Jock. Jock just lay there, well wrapped up with Tatters peeping out from under the sleeping bag, which caused some amusement to the passers-by. It seemed that Tatters had kept him going but I realised now that his life was slowly ebbing away.

His voice was no more than a faint whisper now, and I knew it was close to the end.

"Don't leave me. Don't let me go alone lad."

"I'm here;" I sobbed silently holding him as tight as I could without causing him any more pain. "I'm here and here I'll stay. I promise you that. You have my word." I said so choked with emotion that I could hardly get out the simplest words.

"Good lad. Oh the pain," he twisted in torment.

I knew the time had come to seek medical help and I had asked Maura's advice.

"Having to leave the little dog would kill him," she said. "We wouldn't want him to die of a broken heart but I agree it's time to call an ambulance. In the meantime I think it's best to make him as warm and comfortable as possible. I will give you some medicine for his chest and more sleeping bags. These people are loners and more hardy than you think and find it very difficult to cope with the hospital situation. I have seen it many times, the distress it causes when they are put in a confined space surrounded by strangers, but on the other hand I think Jock is too far gone to resist it. He needs medical help as soon as possible." She dialled 999 from her office and I hurried back to the cardboard."

Jock now had difficulty in getting his breath. He was making a few inaudible sounds, snatching at the pillow with his worn hands. He had come back from the brink before. We were sure he was immortal. But not this time. He was flailing around, his eyes stinging with tears. Gasping for breath a new wave of pain flowed through his emaciated frame. He gave a shudder, convulsed and a little blood flowed from his mouth. I heard him groan and realised that he was very seriously ill.

It was the final night of his life. Sirens sounded and lights flashed as the ambulance parked just outside on the street, a few yards away from Jock. I quickly directed them to the place where he lay, now in an unconscious state. When the first paramedic pulled back the sleeping bag, Tatters leapt out from under the thick layers and bounded across the path where he stood growling.

"My God, what was that?" one of the paramedics jumped backwards.

They loosened his shirt to help him breathe. A small drop of the medicine I had given him earlier dribbled out of the side of his mouth. His eyes opened and closed in a glazed fashion. I realised vaguely that this was serious. Jock was breathing his last. One of the men came across and spoke quietly to me.

"You know we will have to take him to the hospital but we will stabilise his breathing first." I just nodded and at this point. I knew that Jock wouldn't have the energy to resist. His arms hung helplessly by his sides. He muttered something and his breathing was laboured. Perspiration ran down his face and tatty grey locks of hair hung across the side of his face.

The paramedics continued to administer first aid. Jock stirred slowly and emitted a few garbled sounds with short snatchers of breath. His tongue was dry and a sort of hissing. wheezing sound came from his chest. Big Ben struck three like a mournful death toll. Just then Tatters gave a faint and piteous cry. The scruffy little bundle had now crouched on the ground near where Jock lay. Jock was little more than breathing. The sick man had lost all his strength and his will to live. The pain was so intense he couldn't breathe and his face contorted but he gave a faint cry, "Edie. Edie."

"What is it Jock?" I asked.

His hand clutched a dirty piece of paper, which no one had seen before. I reached down and took it from him.

"My sister Edie," he gasped and these were his last words.

At that moment I thought of Dylan Thomas's elegy for his dying father. When Maura discovered my love for poetry, she gave me a small book of Thomas's poetry. This poem "Do not go Gentle into that good night" was addressed to Thomas's father as he lay on his death bed. Like Thomas, I felt anger and rage and an outburst of protest against the inevitability of death. There was the realisation that where they go, we cannot follow. But there was also the inevitability that all men whether wise, good, carefree or serious must face death and have the same final struggle into what Thomas calls that 'good night'. The one certainty which we must all face is death whether we are in the warm bed of a mansion or just lying here in the cardboard.

There was a chill in the air as I held Tatters when they placed old Jock on the stretcher. The little dog gave a soft whining sound. He didn't want to be parted from his master. I lifted him gently. It was the darkest hour of the night just before the dawn.

I would inform Jock's sister and help her with funeral arrangements if she wanted me to.

Tatters jumped back down from my arms and had a run backwards and forwards sniffing the ground. Then he trotted over to lick my hand. His tail wagged for the first time bringing a tear to my eye. Had he already forgotten his old master or decided that I was now his master and that life had to go on. The sky cleared and I lifted Tatters up in my arms and wiping the tears from my eyes, pointed to the brightest star in the sky.

"Do you see that Tatters? He's just gone away home," I said. He'll be waiting for you. And me."

Homeless on earth, had Jock gone to a better place as they always said in eulogies? Was he happier now? But I knew he was at peace.

The moon disappeared behind a cloud. A dark shadow had been cast over our world.

Chapter 17

I had always welcomed the intimate atmosphere of the Shelter, warm food and hot drinks, and the days I used to listen to old Len's conversation which often took me travelling all around the world. I wondered how Len was getting on in North Yorkshire and if I would ever see him again.

"This is a warm place on a cold day," I used to tell Kate but looking all around I was quickly aware of Kate's absence. It was one of my worst days, a day of absences and emptiness. I looked around for Sr. Gabriel but she was in the back kitchen making sandwiches. I approached Amy, another of the volunteers.

"Is Kate here today?"

"No luv. She has left."

"You mean she has gone home early." I thought she may have had an appointment or something. With her teaching commitments all week, she would probably have to fit in this sort of thing at the weekend.

"No luv. She wasn't in today. She has left the Shelter for good."

This was the greatest shock I had had since my first day at the Shelter. I just sat there staring at my food, wondering why Kate had left. "Had she been reprimanded for her over-familiarity with me?" I wondered.

"Surely not! That's not Maura's style." I told myself.

I had arrived in a jubilant mood, hoping to restore some of my confidence. Kate was my guiding light, my life line. But Kate had gone. She had always lifted my spirits and given me new hope.

"How could she do this," I thought, "without telling me." But then why should she tell me. I was no more special than anyone else. Just one more of the homeless. I was filled with emptiness and disappointment. Somehow she had been part of my life. We had liked each other or so I thought. Even Maura had noticed it. But it wasn't true. I had been under an illusion.

Maura called me into her office afterwards.

I had been sailing into a bright new future but now it was all falling apart. There had been so many set-backs, the ladies in the children's playground, the abusive language on my busking patch, the tragedy of Monika's disappearance and the sadness of Jock's death. And now the absence of Kate! It was all weighing down on top of me.

"I seem to be taking one step forward and two backwards all the time," I told Maura.

"You have had a lot of set-backs and I know how Jock's death must have affected you."

"It's just one set-back after another," I told her.

"Yes I know. Some people seem to get more hardships in life than others. I have got a little book I must give you, "When bad things happen to good people."

"Well no. That is not for me. Bad things are happening to me because I am a bad person. I still haven't recovered from Helen's death and I was the cause of it." But Maura had shown me that the guilt I was suffering was not real guilt or sustainable. I would be able to move on.

She held my hand warmly and looked into my eyes. She was so moved and I could tell that she was saddened by Jock's death and had felt these set-backs very deeply.

"The thing you have got to try and hold on to is your reason," her eyes were brimming with tears, but she snatched the tissues and wiped them away.

She spoke quietly. Hers was the voice that was going to set me free. She would eventually guide me towards a different, and a better way of life. But right now all seemed lost.

"You have been through some dark times in your life but believe me there is light at the end of the tunnel."

Maura had proven to be such a positive, life-changing force in my life.

But I didn't think I would pull through this time. Without Kate there was no light at the end of the tunnel.

I thanked Maura and promised to speak with her again and let her know how things were going.

This had been one of the lowest days of my life. Kate's absence had added to my grief. I needed to release some the emotions building up within me, I didn't feel like singing. Picking up my violin from Richard's apartment, I had a strong urge to play some Beethoven. From his music I could hear the voice of love. I was mourning the love of Kate. Beethoven had written some astonishing works considering his own failed attempt to learn the violin. I was in a turbulent mood but needed the beauty and tranquillity Beethoven had given the world. I tried to capture the serene, flowing melodies that pervade a lot of his instrumental works.

There was so much sadness. Kate had filled the void left in my life after I had been the cause of Helen's death. I was now mourning both. I knew I would never see Helen again, and Kate's sudden departure was still a mystery to me. Tears started to fall from my eyes but I didn't care if passers-by noticed. The music came to a graceful end and I loosened the bow and wrapped my beloved violin up gently and carefully in its soft folds of red velvet and prepared to leave. My violin was my only love now.

An old man came forward, leaned over and dropped another coin at my feet. "I've never heard anything so beautiful," he said. "I used to play. But not like that. Good luck son." That old man had done a lot to raise my morale but as I lay in my cold bed that night with Tatters snuggling down into my sleeping bag. I gave a little sigh.

"It's alright Tatters. I understand. We have both loved and lost." I held the pebble in my hand. I could trace the outline of my name. This was all I had to show. The warmth in my heart had been reduced to this cold stone.

But Kevin was not alone. The dark, sinister figure with watchful eyes, just stood still, like in a trance, looking down from the bridge and across to the cardboard with the glow of a cigarette standing out in the deep, inky blackness.

Chapter 18

The next time I went back to the Shelter, a surprise awaited me. Len was back after only two weeks up North. A small group sat around his table and there they were sorting out the nations' problems. Suddenly Len looked up at me.

"I thought we weren't going to see you again" I said.

"It was bloody cold up there. I couldn't stand it."

"But what about the grandchildren?"

"Don't ask. Kids nowadays are so over-indulged. There is a house full of toys. They have so many toys they could start a toy store. I was tripping over plastic toys all over the place. I nearly broke my neck on the stairs when I trod on a toy train."

"Well you won't have that problem here." I thanked the volunteers and went off then for my run. I knew I would be hearing lots more about the grandchildren at a later date.

"Poor old Len," I thought.

I still had that vein of stern discipline running through my nature and ran across the bridge towards the South Bank. I had always taken my duties very seriously and now I took up my daily routine as though my life depended on it. I ran until I reached the book stalls where Tony stopped me in my tracks.

"Hi there Kev, where have you been?" Tony ran one of the book stalls on the South Bank, another refuge in my lonely life, and we had become good friends.

"Here, there and everywhere," I suppose my gloomy look told Tony that there was something wrong and that I needed a bit of cheering up.

"How is Dickens coming on?"

"Oh, he's been put to rest. I have taken to the Dickens rambles through the city instead." We talked a bit more about Dickens and some of his works. I likened him to William Blake but I was surprised that Tony was not big into poetry.

"Hey man you know more about this city than I do," Tony said. "What will it be next time? I have a clean copy of Lawrence's 'Sons and Lovers'. He is writing almost a century after Austen and Dickens. Have you read much Lawrence?"

"No definitely not. It was frowned upon in my school even though the ban had been lifted. But that only made some of the students keener. But I hadn't time anyway." It was then that I realised that my life in Cambridge had afforded very little time for personal reading. There had been all the academic texts, law case studies to work on but come to think of it they were thrillers in their own right but sadly real life thrillers, not the work of fiction.

"I've put aside a clean copy for you," Tony said.

"I'd like to try it. Thanks." I rummaged in my pockets for some change.

"Forget it. Consider it a gift from me this time. Maybe you can buy me a brandy when you are rich and famous" Tony joked before turning to another customer. I nodded towards him as I left.

I was acutely aware that Tony was one of the few persons outside the Shelter who had shown me respect.

I thought of Tony's words, 'a clean copy'. Surely any filthy old copy would be good enough.

I sat on a bench overlooking the river and began reading right away. I had become an avid reader, consuming books faster than I could find them and I was thankful for this new hobby because it took up a good share of the long lonely days. I thought if everyone enjoyed reading the word boredom would be eliminated for our vocabulary. The tension was lifting now and my books were my new companions. My life now fitted together like a jig-saw puzzle.

But as he walked back down the embankment, Kevin was not alone. A dark figure leaned over the railings, with watchful eyes in a face lit by the glimmer of a cigarette.

Chapter 19

It was a sweltering hot day in June and Sr. Gabriel had installed two large cooling fans in the dining room. She passed cold drinks and sandwiches around the tables. There didn't seem to be much demand for hot food. I sat next to Len and he seemed to have a new grievance with the world.

"There are disputes every day. Hot weather seems to bring out the worst in people, particularly in relation to their neighbours" he said. "People are never satisfied. One minute they are moaning about the cold and now it's the heat eating into them. Children playing too noisily, loud music through open windows, barbecue smoke in gardens next door. Occasionally neighbour disputes build up into court cases. Sometimes next door neighbours are not very neighbourly," he gave a sort of chuckle.

"Particularly over property boundaries. Yes... and often over abuse and violence. But you know sometimes a direct friendly approach can usually sort things out without police being called round or an ASBO being served. People should talk to each other, taking the initiate themselves. No need to shift responsibilities to the police. They have enough to do."

We talked on for a while and when the volunteers started clearing the tables, we went on our separate ways. I walked along the cooling water of the Thames. Walking over the bridge I gazed down at the river below. Then I carried out my daily routine, my running, my reading and busking. In the evenings Kate, to my great delight, usually turned up to listen to my music but sometimes she had a sad expression on her face. When I had finished we began going to one of the coffee bars along the river. I was beginning to see the reason, or hoped it was the reason, why she had left the Shelter. Now that she had left, she wasn't breaking any rules so there was no need for me to feel guilty. Before I knew it I was having long conversations with Kate, about the weather, about events in the newspaper and I started to talk about my concerns over Monika's disappearance.

"Don't worry. She wasn't my girlfriend." I wanted Kate to be sure of that.

"I was supposed to be protecting her. Keeping any eye out for her," I said and Kate saw the sadness in my eyes. She squeezed my shoulder. She knew I needed to talk. I had bottled up my emotions for too long. There were too many strangulated memories. I needed to grieve and Kate was a good listener.

She took my hand, "Go on you need to let it out." She was starting to mean the world to me. Whatever I was doing, whether eating or brushing my teeth, I was dreaming about her all the time. I looked up at her and couldn't believe how strong she was, rushing to see me every day after work, not having eaten and still with a smile on her face. My life was much richer for having her by my side. Somehow it felt like I'd been given a chance to get back on track. Kate had the power of transforming me. She made my life worth living. She had a magical quality and I seemed to bring it out in her.

Then quite out of the blue, Kate said, "I have got to be honest with you. I have had my own sad story too although it is very different from yours. I have just come through a very painful divorce after two years of an extremely stressful marriage. My mistake was marrying the wrong person. I thought I was in love with Harry but all he wanted was power and control. He was manipulative and a bully, suspicious of everything I did.

"Oh I'm so sorry Kate," was all I could say.

But I still had my reservations. I knew she would be happier with a normal person. And yet from our first conversations, there was a trust and understanding between us. As time went on we spent most evenings in a cafe or at the cinema, vaguely dreaming that any moment the answers would suddenly hit me? Did Kate really like me or was it just pity or sympathy. Was I out of my mind? She is not going to fall for a homeless victim when she has so much going for her in her own career. Even on the most desperately grim day she gave me hope. She always cheered me up, looking stunning with that endearing smile. I wanted to get to know her better. Each time I saw her, my face as well as my heard would light up.

Thanks to Kate I had rediscovered the good side of human nature. I had begun to place my trust and faith in people again. She had a profound effect on my life. We were already getting too involved and I wasn't sure where it was leading.

As we walked along one evening, Kate suddenly said, "I think I saw him over there by that pillar."

"Who?"

"The Boston Wanderer."

"Surely you would think he would have given up by now," I said. We walked on not giving him another thought.

I accompanied her over to Waterloo station on her way home. I remember one particular evening after we had said goodbye, I went back along South Bank. I wanted to have the freedom of the wind, the freedom of the elements. I had discovered the secret of happiness or I thought I had. There was a new sense of belonging in my life. Do you believe in love at first sight? I was beginning to think so. From the first moment I saw her, I was drawn to her so deeply, so immediately, a strong magnet pulling, that I hoped was real and meant to last forever, someone who would make even the mundane things in life seem poignant.

She was the joy of my life who cured all illnesses, all of my senses, removed all my despair. Now that I had freed myself from all negative thoughts, she gave me new dreams of the future. I had emerged into a spiritual world of beauty and wisdom. My time with Kate was an oasis in the desert of my barren soul. She had taught me to listen to my heart. I had found love and riches. A rare treasure. But I needed to find out for sure. We held hands. Kate wore sunglasses and a summer hat which was both endearing and odd. She looked a bit like a movie star, the way she was beginning to enjoy everything, full of the joys of life. When we were together even the smallest thing took on significance. Every touch brought pleasure

I took her hand gently as we said goodbye at the station. Then as the whistle blew for her train, she said in the softest voice, "You are the light of my life." Or at least that is what I thought she said.

"The man in the mirror has become my friend," I told myself. "You must stop selling yourself short."

Kate was a realist. She had helped me step back inside a new comfort zone.

I began to acknowledge that I needed to come to terms with my past, embrace the future and stop procrastinating. I had found a new courage.

"Decisions shouldn't be put off. They should be made now. Others had tried to cram my mistakes down my throat." Kate's happiness and enthusiasm were contagious. Life was worth living again. I needed to create a new life. We could fix this together.

"Why so cheerful this morning," Maura said as I walked back into the Shelter.

"Oh just because I'm full of the joys of life. I'm going to leave the streets soon."

"I think I know what all that is about. Kate has told me quite a lot."

I sat up with a jolt. "Yes Kate! I have had a lot of contact with her since she left the Shelter. We were always best friends and she has told me everything. I think there is a future there for you two. I told her to take things easy but she seems to have made up her mind.

I had the answers to many of my questions and couldn't wait to meet Kate that evening.

"I have been friends with Kate's parents for years," Maura went on. "In fact our children grew up together and we used to go on holiday to the beach every summer. That was until my husband died. Then my life changed completely. Tom died from a heart attack at sixty-two. But the worst was still to come. My son developed lung cancer. And he never smoked in his life. Isn't it ironic? After two years he passed away, so you see there are parallels between his life and yours. He was my only child and best friend, the person I relied on."

"At the time I couldn't face people. I gave up my job in the bank and I just stayed indoors all the time. But someone suggested bereavement counselling and this was the best thing that could have happened. They encouraged me to get out there and take up some new hobbies or a part-time job. I did more than that. I took a course in counselling and later worked with Alcoholic Anonymous. And after that I trained and for six years. I worked with the Samaritans and I think this is where I found my true vocation. I felt I was doing something useful for the community instead of hiding away and nursing my own grief."

"I think this is where I developed my listening skills, giving people time to form their words, allowing people to unravel their thoughts especially if it had been a long time since they shared their feelings with anyone. I found that people could feel embarrassed to talk to anyone and I could feel the pain behind their struggle, that they could see no future and wanted to end it all."

"I let people pour out their feelings, their anger, their frustration, their pain, their despair. Telling people to pull themselves together only puts more pressure on a person who is already feeling powerless and overwhelmed. I learned to keep my questions open and gentle. We need to assure people that no matter how bad things get, they will be listened to in confidence. To begin with, they just want to get all their emotions out."

"In my work I have learned things about myself and others that will, I hope, serve me for the rest of your life. It was a need to give people the time and space to express all their feelings, without prejudice, without judgment. Finally I came here as a voluntary worker. I have found the work here very fulfilling even though there are times when it can be quite demanding. You know something? The first time I met you, I thought you looked just like my son."

"But I'm sure he didn't look anything like me."

"Well actually he did.... after your first shower and shave," she laughed.

"After all you have told me, I intend to come back and we can have a long chat. Or better still, I will take you out for a meal one evening."

"That would be delightful," she said.

When I was leaving Maura whispered in my ear.

"You have found a fantastic girl, and she's not doing too badly either. Good Luck to you both."

She had always been sensitive, warm and supportive, without ever being judgmental, but after all she had told me, I started to admire her even more. Despite all her own adversity, she gave her time and energy to supporting layabouts like myself."

Chapter 20

I thought I would give busking one last try. I had wanted to play my violin previously to relieve me of some of the tension and emotion which were pouring through my veins but my music was no longer an escape from the problems around me or my own tragedies. It had now become a celebration. The first time I collected the violin from Richard's flat. I was surprised to find that the strings were intact and it barely needed tuning. It had been grieving, lying waiting for someone to bring it back to life, to fill the world with its wonderful sound. I picked the violin from its case, adjusted the bridge and tightened the bow. That day I was haunted by '*Bolero*', Revel's masterpiece.

I was playing long slow chords, then on open strings and finally warming up scales. This time my music was just for myself, not for any particular audience. And ironically it was at these times that I benefited financially. It was not the usual busking type music and it was at the most unexpected moments that the money kept pouring in. I tried to play with grace and sensitivity to convey the richness of the violin to the audience which had now gathered around me.

I produced a full-blooded vibrato like I had never played before resounding through the delicate rosewood making the instrument cry with emotion and the money kept coming. I imagined I was surrounded by the full orchestra from my position as first violinist. The theme was languid and mournful. As the final notes faded away, with satisfaction I loosened the strings on the bow, stroked the violin gently and put it to bed wrapped in the soft fabric.

Suddenly I got an enormous shock when I recognised the person coming towards me. It was none other than Andrew Arkwright my music teacher and conductor of the school orchestra, probably making his way into the Royal Festival Hall.

I had vaguely remembered seeing his name on some programme of events but hadn't bargained on seeing him here.

"Is this what you're doing with your music and all your talents?" I was self-conscious and ashamed. This had been one of the most embarrassing moments since I went on the streets.

"You know it doesn't sound quite the same with only one instrument," Andrew said sarcastically. He had never forgiven me for deserting the orchestra and he was outraged that I had now become a waster.

"You could have been first violinist in the London Philharmonic or any other decent orchestra if you had followed a music career."

"I would have loved that but...."

I was cut off abruptly. Andrew dropped a five pound note into the case and sauntered off, without a backward glance. The insult had really got the better of me. I was angry, hurt, insulted. Even if I wanted to I could not have gone on playing. I walked back to Richard's apartment to return the violin. Richard was there lending a sympathetic ear but I could feel he was thinking 'I told you so'. After a coffee and a long chat, I wandered out on the streets wearily. I ran, pounding the pavement, running away from everyone, the past, the present, my guilt. My confusion!

But this time it was only a small set-back. The next day, I was back on form. My violin was one of my cherished possessions. Made from only the best materials, rosewood, spruce and maple with ebony fingerboard, pegs and tailpiece, by a master craftsman, a gift from my parents after I was accepted into the National Youth Orchestra.

"Made by a master to produce the best sound for a master player and it's up to the master player," my father said.

The instrument was light with the most resonant qualities. I tuned up, and cleansed all the resin gently with a soft cloth, tightened the horsehair bow, rubbed the hairs with some new resin. How good it was to play, not to work at it, to play for my own pleasure with no need to convey anything to anyone outside. Finally I made another small adjustment to the tuning and the bridge. Roy Graves, another of my music teachers had me memorise Vivaldi's 'Four Seasons' for a school concert during my final year. Roy had also pleaded with me to pursue a musical career but I had opted for a law degree which pleased my father greatly. "A chip off the old block" was his way of boasting about my success.

I drew the bow over the strings and played like I had never played before. It was all there in my sub-conscious waiting to come out. I played with such vigour trying to emulate the music of Nigel Kennedy, one of the world's leading violin virtuosos. More money poured into the violin case.

It was a week trying to recapture my own love for the violin. The following day I found myself humming some of Mahler's intensely beautiful songs. He drove himself and poured his feelings into his music. In contrast, I kept running away from my problems but I could now feel the return of the great intensity in my own music.

Although I had my own resources to draw on, I could not bring myself to use any of my parents' money or even dip into my own savings. Not yet! I suppose this was a sort of penance for my guilt. If my mates at the Shelter had been aware of my circumstance they would surely have tried to have me certified as totally insane.

Chapter 21

When I got back to the cardboard, Mahmud was standing by the wall and being searched by two policemen. There were other policemen standing next to a large police van on the road. In an instant the policemen had thrown him to the ground and were on top of him. They pinned his arms behind him in handcuffs. Mahmud was screaming with all his strength. He had been dealt a hard blow in life. The whole world conspired against him. I knew he was in serious trouble. I had often seen money change hands, not much but the users and the suppliers were desperate. His eyes now blazed with sudden anger and he screamed out in a deranged voice.

"We're banging you up," they said and manhandled him against the wall, his hands behind his back. He protested violently and vigorously. They frisked him. Nothing in his raincoat pockets, nothing in his shoes so they pushed up his sleeves and the legs of his trousers, looking for needle marks.

"You're a drug dealer," one of them said.

"No, I'm not. Honestly!" He sounded like the small boy explaining to his cruel father to spare himself further punishment.

"I smoke heroin but I'm not a dealer."

They dragged him roughly towards the waiting police van.

"We are going to lock you up and examine what you have to say a bit more closely."

Mahmud kicked one of the officers on the shins. Kicking and screaming, he had now gone berserk. His violence had escalated through his dependence on drink and drugs but it had all stemmed back to his childhood. He had finally retaliated against years of abuse. He had passed into such drink-induced oblivion that he had no recollection of what was going on around him. Sadly Mahmud was beginning to become like the disagreeable and aggressive father he despised. Full of anger and despair, he burst into tears. I had tried to get him into a treatment centre but every time I suggested it Mahmud flew into a rage.

The scene made me upset and angry, despite all his previous abuse and aggression towards me. I saw the look of despair and hopelessness on Mahmud's face but sadly he was only one in a city of addicts.

"Home is where the hurt is." I had heard that slogan so many times in some advertisement for child protection. Mahmud had never stood a chance. He had found himself deeply discouraged, having experienced one rejection after another. He just stood there dejected but then something wild came out of his throat. It was a wail.

"I remembered the day he took a screwdriver," he told Monika about his fear of his father, "Held it up in front of my face and threatened to gouge my eyes out and strangle me. He was shouting, pulling my hair and ranting. I was begging him to stop and thought he was going to kill me, so terrified I felt suicidal and thought it would be best to kill myself painlessly before he mercilessly murdered me."

I remembered other conversations with Monika, "One night my father finally snapped, picked up a hot iron and held it on my arm. For years I had taken the beatings and abuse. One night he pushed me against the wall and started banging my head with his fist. He slapped me across the face. On another occasion he broke my finger by twisting my hand and on that same night he snatched a cup of black coffee and threw it at me. I still have a scar where it scalded my leg. I couldn't see an end of the violence."

They bundled him into the van and I heard sirens as they drove down the embankment. "He will get more, love affection and freedom in prison that he'd ever had at home," I thought. For the first time he will eat a decent meal and have somewhere to lay his head.

The only problem he would ever admit was that of how he would get hold of his next fix. He was incapable of recognising just how bizarre his life had become and did not recognise how ill he was. I wondered if people saw him in this light too. I had to attribute his sense of failure to some weakness, not of body but of mind and spirit. It was obvious that there was a wide and varied spectrum of problems related to alcohol and drugs. Mahmud had sunk to the bottom of the pit. He suffered memory losses, hallucinations, fits, and damage to his health and he hurled verbal or physical abuse at anyone who crossed his path. He had no way of s knowing the damage he was doing.

When I thought of all the things he had told Monika, I realised that his condition involved the collapse of self-esteem and the building of negative defence systems that alienated him from society and life. His patterns of drugs and bout-drinking were so destructive.

He had told Monika how his violently alcoholic father had experienced the same drunken binges and his life had spiralled into hopeless alcoholism. He was a brutal drunk who beat his son and his mother during his alcoholic rages. Mahmud said he was six or seven when his father first hit him. One night he threw him against a door and cracked one of his ribs. He had lived all his life in fear.

"You never knew what was going to happen next," he told Monika. "There would be an explosion of violence for no apparent reason. He once swiped me round the jaw with a poker and I am still a light sleeper because my father would come home in the early hours and haul me out of bed and hurl me against a wall. There were times when I thought I was going to die. I hated my father.

I felt ashamed when I realised all that Mahmud had gone through when I myself had had such a sheltered life surrounded by love. I was worried and decided to speak with anyone who knew Mahmud and I would go to the police station. The jury will see this case as a helpless, victimised impoverished young man, or as a useless, drug addict. Would Mahmud be able to hold it together?

"Life just isn't fair," I thought.

Chapter 22

I had to get out of this life. Kate had lifted me above the turmoil but I myself was now in the driving seat. I had to make a good life for both of us. But I didn't yet know if Kate was to be part of my future, if I was merely an object of her charity and kindness. Everyone was advising her to take things slowly.

In many ways my life was back on track. I watched other people wandering about their lives, each of them would have huge events in their own families, loves and losses, dark secrets, great joys and great tragedies. I needed to put it into perspective. If they could just enjoy a sunny evening in a beer garden, then surely I could too. I had regained my own identity and thought things through as I played absent-mindedly, the opening chords of a song and some melancholy tunes from the past. I sang sad songs, full of tenderness and delicate warmth.

This was going to be a special night.

"May I spend tonight at your place?" I asked Richard.

"About time! How many times have I tried to persuade you?!"

"Well things are quite different now. Kate has invited me to a concert in the Royal Festival Hall and I don't think it would be appropriate to get washed and dressed in the cardboard," I laughed.

"I'm so happy for you Kevin. I told you it was only a matter to time. Good luck!"

After a shower I stood in front of the bathroom mirror, looking at my reflection as I shaved. I was no longer trapped, and my mind was beginning to function. I lingered in the lounge listening to the radio, sitting on the sofa in Richard's dressing gown having just completed rereading *'The Alchemist'* by Paulo Coelho I was reflecting on my own treasures. It was 15th June and my 30th birthday and Kate arranged the visit to the concert as a celebration. I never thought I would enjoy such happiness again.

That evening I had arranged to meet her coming out from Waterloo station. There she was in a long black dress, with a short white jacket coming out of the station and looking towards where I stood at the other side of the street. I signalled to her that I was coming over but she looked right and left then crossed the road.

"You look ravishing," I told her and kissed her lightly on the cheek.

"And look at you! Happy birthday, Kevin!"

I was in a dark suit, wearing a white shirt and tie and for the first time in ages I felt properly dressed, thanks to Richard giving me a free run of his flat and wardrobe. I took Kate's hand and we walked toward The Royal Festival Hall.

"So where is this Skylon?" Kate asked.

"Just follow me," I said as we went over to the lifts. This was my part of the birthday treat, what they called a pre-theatre champagne dinner. We were shown to our seats especially reserved overlooking the river. After dinner, Kate put her hand in her handbag and produced a small package.

"Happy Birthday!" she said again and handed me the small gift neatly wrapped in gold paper. I just sat there and took a sip from my champagne. I wanted to savour these moments before I opened the gift. It had been a long time since anything like this had happened in my life.

"Oh my goodness," I said, "An i-phone. I will have to get used to all this new technology.

"All paid up and ready to go," she said. Then she called one of the waiters over and asked him to take a picture of the two of us on my new phone, with the river and St. Paul's in the background. I would never forget his moment.

"And I have something for you," I said and took the small box out of my pocket.

"Thank you, but you didn't have to. It's your day, you know."

"I have wanted to do this a long time ago," I told her.

She removed the paper and opened the little box. There, against the dark-blue velvet, was a thin gold chain and a little pendant with a *K* on it. She let her eyes rest on it before she spoke.

"It's lovely," she said as I leant across the table and fastened it around her neck.

"I will love wearing it," she said.

"Glad you like it," I said. She came over and. kissed me on the cheek. The champagne had taken away our inhibitions.

"Time for the concert," Kate reached into her bag for the tickets. We took a lift to the auditorium and immediately were surrounded by people crammed into the bar in their jewels and evening clothes. There was a cool air of prosperity. It was almost time for the concert and the great gleaming foyer still had a few people in it but a bell was chiming repetitively.

An announcement came through the speakers, "Now three minutes left before the start of the concert." We watched the silence all around us as people finished their drinks and started moving up towards the auditorium. Once inside I stared with awe at the big breathless space and the instruments tuning up in the orchestra pit beneath the brightly-lit stage. The conductor inclined his head as the lights gleamed and flickered. Gradually the audience fell silent. Though a familiar sensation was in my heart as I saw the first violinist bow to the audience and take his seat, I understood at this moment, that I was fortunate. Optimism seemed to have caught me unawares. For a moment, I thought I was dreaming. The surroundings had been a distant part of my life.

When the last notes of the orchestra had died away and after the rapturous applause and standing ovation, we stood up and I helped Kate into her jacket.

"Night," she whispered and kissed my forehead as we walked hand-in-hand back towards her taxi. We stood there, both silent, staring at each other for several seconds. I knew there would be many more nights like this. I was overcome with happiness. I kissed her goodnight and as I saw her into her taxi, she raised her head and kissed me again.

"I love you," she whispered. It was so soft that I thought I was dreaming, a long distant dream. I was hugely proud of her and filled with love for her, a love so deep.

As I walked across Hungerford bridge, I couldn't take my eyes off the panorama of the dazzling riverfront and the steady flood of brilliance which illuminated the buildings. I was seeing London in an entirely new light.

Behind him the lights of the Eye wavered slowly through the air and as he walked away a mysterious figure, all in black looked across the expanse of water towards Kevin as he approached Richard's flat. There was the same bright glow of a cigarette shining out of the shadows on the bridge. The same dark figure with a smirk on his face!

I was back at Richard's. "Well tell me all about it" he said handing me a brandy. We talked half the night and I slept in the guest room until mid-morning. Maybe this was the beginning of my new beginning. It had been a long day. A day of enlightenment! The world was no longer black and white. It was all the colours of the rainbow.

Chapter 23

My mind was taken up with Monika's disappearance. I saw her face everywhere before me and tried to imagine she was sleeping here under the cardboard. My running took me to all the usual haunts for the homeless but the search was futile. One day I would return to the cardboard and find her there. I had to believe it. This was one reason I stayed in the cardboard longer than I needed to. I continued to search day and night, through the streets and the darkness of the alleyways. I knew that some women who were brought into Britain for 'sexual exploitation' were so traumatised and ashamed they would probably continue to work as prostitutes. Maybe this was the answer to Monika's disappearance.

"To trail a missing person in London's maze of alleyways is bordering on the impossible," Maura told me. "It happens all the time. People go missing and are never seen again." The hours dragged, but there was no answer. I tried to phone Sara again. Only a long silence on the phone and then the voicemail kicked in.

"The person you are calling is not available... please leave a message." Another day gone in the hopeless search. It was dark, a kind of twilight. There were faint lights coming from the Eye. The people in the pods were barely visible. But regular flashes from cameras indicated that there were many tourists aboard. I looked upward, trying to remain calm, refusing to panic. Another hour passed. I was still pacing up and down but finally decided to lie down again.

Mahmud seemed to have gone too. I had reported Monika as a missing person. The police noted my statement but like Maura said that one more missing person in London could be impossible to find. But it then occurred to me that Mahmud could have been the culprit. Indeed Monika herself could have been the one to have administered the blow on my head. I remembered that it was a soft muffled blow. It could have been administered by a girl of her size. "It is a complete dead end," I thought about the everyday bleakness set in the shady underworld of London.

On my runs, I went around asking the street people under bridges and huddled in doorways. They were welcoming but couldn't offer any help. I'd had no sleep since the previous morning. The early evening had been terrible. Waiting, impossible to relax, too nervous, too tense. I found myself sitting on a bench with my back to the water and eyes fixed on the London Eye.

The next morning I went to the Shelter for one last time, where I was always guaranteed a warm shower and change of clothing and the sheer luxury of having a piping hot drink and listening to Len putting the world to rights. He came and sat next to me and spread the Metro out on the table. For a while we sat there eating in silence.

"The world is a different place," Len said. "I remember the time when art was art. Look at this!" he pointed to an article in the newspaper.

"Have you heard about the controversial creations of this man Damien Hirst?"

"Yes I know he is very famous and very rich," I said.

"Look at this. A shorn sheep sitting on a lavatory sear. I ask you!"

"And another with a hypodermis syringe sticking out of its leg. And scattered on the floor beside the beast is the paraphernalia of a junkie. What's all that about?"

"You know he had something in common with us, a rebellious son, and took to alcohol and drugs. But he gave all that up. You have got to admire him for that."

"Well I don't think much of his art. Look at this one. Another sheep on a lavatory, this time appearing to vomit into a sink with an empty vodka bottle and some scattered pills."

"Presumable some sort of symbolism," I said but I had to admit I didn't know a lot about the art and decided to go along to one of the galleries and find out some more. Maybe I could enlighten Len.

"Umm. They look interesting," I said. "They say the use of living creatures enables Hirst to incorporate an element of movement into his works."

"Interesting? Death is a recurrent theme in Hirst's work. "Money for old rope. That's what I say. He doesn't even do the work himself. Apparently he just comes up with the ideas but never lifts a finger to produce them. He has a team of people in this so-called art studio putting all these wild ideas together. Look at this, corpses of flies and a decaying cow's head. How can you say that is interesting?"

"He's probably saying something about something important," I said mulling it over in my own mind and determined to find out more.

"He has an obsession with death," Len said. Just then Sr. Gabriel came over to clear the tables.

"Ah go on with you Len. You are depressing us all with your talk about death. You are frightening people."

"It's not me Sister. Look at this!" He pointed to the article. This man Hirst is stark raving mad. His works are lumps of dead animals. What about all the young artists who don't get a look in?"

"Maybe you have a point there Len. But cheer up. It might never happen." Sr. Gabriel laughed and went on with her work.

"I think he is getting us to explore into the deep profundities of life and death," I said and he wants to provoke a reconsideration of how we respond to death in his works."

But Len wasn't listening. He went on reading the article.

"There is a debate here as to whether Hirst's displays are in fact 'art'. But there is no need for debate. How could you call that art? It's a strange form of art, if you ask me. This work is a far cry from the wonderful artists we see in the National Gallery, Van Gough, Leonardo da Vinci, Monet. Wonderful works and wonderful to look at. And what about Michelangelo and the Sistine Chapel and all that?"

"Real art. That's what I say." He turned away from the Damien Hirst centre spread.

"What next?" I wondered.

Chapter 24

I was still dreaming of a different future, but trapped in the present even more so with Monika's disappearance. In my distress, I had gone from the cardboard to Richard's apartment.

"You're not responsible for all the missing persons in London," Richard said.

"But Monika is different. Like family in a way." Her disappearance was driving me frantic with worry. My whole life and few possessions were in Richard's flat, except for the pebble. I carried that everywhere in my pocket. I already had a considerable collection of my favourite CD classics and a few books on music. Sometimes I felt it was strange that my music had been amongst my treasured possessions.

In amongst the books I had my one favourite picture taken at my graduation, of my mother, father and Helen. If I looked at the picture they all came to life and Helen moved a little towards me to hold my hand. She was warm and loving then and I could not have imagined the tragedy which would envelop me within four years of this happy day. In the picture mother was reaching over to fix my gown and father stood tall and proud without moving a muscle. I still had not got the courage to put the photo on top of the shelf.

It was after midnight when I left Richard's. I stood by the river looking up at the Eye. My head ached and I really did not feel well. I had been trying to look out for Monika and had failed her. Perhaps there was some explanation about her disappearance but the knock on my head had been real. I was still lightheaded.

"Are you alright?" Sr. Gabriel asked when I reached the dining room the next morning.

"Thank you," I said but I just sat there quietly in my favourite corner and made my way quietly up the narrow steps and back onto the street.

That evening I started to walk along the riverside. The Eye was moving slowly, its huge bulk standing out ominously against the night sky. Lifeless and all-seeing. I stood on the embankment. My heart was pounding as I stood cradling Monika's phone in my hand.

I dialled and finally reached Sara. "Any news," I asked.

"No nothing. I was just going to phone you to ask you the same question."

She didn't know anything and was as alarmed as I was. We agreed to meet again at her place in Rotherhithe.

"Let's think of all the possibilities," I said. "There was violence in the way I had been manhandled. This was by someone who was capable of anything."

Maybe she knew more than she was saying but I didn't think so. There was something trusting about her. For one thing she had allowed me to visit her in her own home.

She hesitated for a long time. "The last day I saw her was the night before she disappeared," Sara said.

"What did she way?"

"Nothing unusual."

"Any indication that she had plans to more out?" I asked.

"No, she would have told me. I was the only friend she had."

That night I continued to search for Monika but I had become more and more concerned. The traffic accelerated after the traffic lights. It was a freezing cold night. I zipped up my anorak and pulled the collar up over my ears. I kept running to warm myself searching every nook and cranny.

Chapter 25

I could now talk openly with Kate about my mother and father and about Helen. She was the only person I could confide in, apart from Maura and Richard, since Helen's death and my guilt was beginning to fade. People had told me I was not responsible for my Father's death or Helen's. Sitting there, looking at me, I imagined she could decipher the strained look around my eyes, the silences, the way I seemed to retreat inside my own skin.

But I had to be careful not to burden her too much with my own problems. She needed space to help overcome her own problems but she still tried to cheer me up.

"I can see your eyes begin to crease with a faint smile and I would like to keep them like that," she said. She wanted me to be happy, for my face to lose that haunted, faraway, forlorn look I saw so often in the mirror, a face that spoke of silent pain.

"Things will change," she said. "Life will go on. We are all part of some great cycle, some pattern. There is a bigger picture, a brighter future," she said calmly

The slim white coffin flashed before my eyes, a simple spray of pink roses on top from my parents and my single red rose. Helen's father stood at the lectern and delivered the eulogy but now it was all a dim, distant memory. I held the pebble in the palm of my hand and told Kate the whole story, how Helen had come around in her jogging suit, to make last-minute preparations for our wedding, had given me the pebble and sat chatting. Richard, who was to be my best man, was there too. We talked and laughed about preparations, dresses and screeches.

Then mother came in from the kitchen. "I have just been listening to the radio and I don't want to alarm you, but a storm is blowing up. In fact the rain has already started to come down."

"I'll run you home," father was already on his feet and walking towards Helen.

"No you take my car," I had said. "Dad will drop me round later. I just need to finish off a few things with Richard. I'll take the car back home later."

"No problem. I have driven this car a few times before," Helen said.

"We kissed each other goodbye and then...." he hesitated.

"Shh, don't go on if it's too painful," Kate said.

"It's ok. I want you to know everything. The rain got heavier after she left and began to come down in torrents.

"I'm glad Helen's not out in that jogging suit," Richard said and we all laughed.

Apparently dazzled by an oncoming car on a sharp bend, almost immediately the car seemed uncontrollable. Helen braked suddenly on the wet road, braking and skidding, across the road and finally careering across the bank somersaulting down into a small ravine and crashing into a tree at the bottom. Stillness formed and a strange silence overtook the scene, engines stopped, horns hushed. Within the space of less than a minute that absolute irresistible force had taken its hold on the time and place. It had disrupted the present, distorted the future, replaced order with chaos and changed my life forever. When Helen died part of my world died with her." I sat there motionless and Kate waited.

After a long silence, I told her that everyone had consoled me. "She probably hadn't felt a thing," they said.

"No she wouldn't," Kate held my hand and waited.

"The verdict was accidental death, but I continued to blame myself. I could have dropped her home and been back in ten minutes but instead I had to live with this lifetime of guilt."

In my mind, I was back there at the scene. I saw the black crags, the far Pennines and the swirl in the river. Birds soared overhead. At this moment some church clock chimed in the valley. The light was fading more gently than before. I saw the misty fields, cottages with lamps in the windows but all was still.

"It's ok. You are here now," Kate squeezed my hand.

Chapter 26

When Big Jim arrived in the cardboard, it was in a quiet way. He was a gentle giant, huge in stature but when he walked, he was almost invisible. He was a private person, deeply religious and reserved and had come from a close, loving Afro-Caribbean family. He had only been there for two weeks and hadn't bothered anyone. He seemed lonely to me, lonely and forgotten. Many of his peers fell into a life of crime, drugs and the street gang culture which had blighted the tough inner-city areas where he lived. I looked at the sad face and knew that Jim was different. He didn't fall into the world of drugs and alcohol. During his time in the cardboard as we walked to the Shelter, Jim told me his sad story.

"I worked hard at school and tried to channel my energies into self-improvement," he told me. "I wanted to secure a steady job. If someone had tried to drag me into an argument, I would have laughed and walked away." He had planned to become a lawyer but suffered a history of ill-health following a car accident which had forced him to give up his London studies.

He was trying to avoid trouble and had walked through back streets away from the chaos but he was spotted by his attackers. The gang wearing bandanas and hoods leapt out from nowhere and chased after their victim into the cardboard. Jim turned and stared in shock, tears in his eyes, crying but trying to hide it. His attackers stood in front of him, an unmoving wall of black. Black hoods and black scarves around their faces. All I could see were eyes. Four pairs of eyes. They were all blacked-out from top to toe, and waving knives which meant they were going to cause serious trouble.

When I heard the commotion, I watched in disbelief with growing fear and growing horror. I crouched lower where I couldn't be seen. I knew I was powerless and wouldn't stand a chance against a group of thugs this size. Powerless even to raise the alarm. I quietly dialled 999 and hoped I wouldn't be heard. Fear rushed through my body, mixed with rage, desperation and helplessness.

The violence kicked off. The first crazed man flicked out his knife and attempted to slice open Jim's throat. The others lunged forward towards him with their knives, screaming oaths in terror and fury, curses raging in their voices. Jim screamed in despair. He howled with pain and his scream's rose up to the starry sky. The attack was driven by racial disharmony, a group of immature, ill-educated teenagers, shouting and swearing and calling out racial abuse with every stab, "Paki.... wogs.... The wogs jump the job queues.... cheat on the social.... take our jobs." Jim's cries of agony travelled across the endless expanse of water. He finally let out a howl of terror so intense and painful his scream pierced the cool night air, shrill and terrible as it echoed through the trees, down the bank and then it abruptly stopped. The gang shuffled of laughing. A deathly silence.

I stood gazing at a pool of blood, Jim's life draining down the cold slabs. I pushed my way through the debris and the crowds which had gathered and tried to stop the blood flow although I knew the wounds were fatal. People stood in horror dialling on their mobiles. Blood was seeping through Jim's jeans in a dozen places. He had been stabbed to death, lying on the ground in a pool of his own blood. He did not die of an illicit morphine overdose. He was not a heroin addict and had never been. He was murdered for no just reason. Jim was lying dead in the path and beside him was the drug paraphernalia typical of a heroin addict. He had been stabbed and then surrounded by planted evidence of drug-taking. I was bending over him trying desperately again to stem the blood flow, as I waited for the police and ambulance. A thick line of blood ran down the path. At the sound of the sirens, the rest of the curious crowd had scattered and I stood alone near a pool of Jim's blood.

Five minutes later there were sirens blaring, death lit up the night sky as police cars and an ambulance flashed their blinding lights through the square surrounding Jim's large, lifeless body. People were pushed aside to allow an ambulance to enter. Men lifted out a stretcher.

The officers from the Crime Squad arrived and took over. Paramedics declared him dead at the scene of the crime. The uniformed police had blocked off a large rectangle around the body. Photographs were taken and the body was transported to the morgue at four o'clock in the morning, the unearthly pre-dawn hour. Then the various emergency services left, one after the other.

"This is all for you Jim," I whispered to myself as the ambulance pulled out onto the main road. "You have never had such attention in your life." I wiped away the tears with the back of my hand.

I walked away from the scene, stumbling along the bank. There were spots of blood on my jeans. I was wearing part of Jim's life, little red drops of Jim's precious blood. My head was spinning for the next few days. I felt a real mixture of emotions. I slept fitfully that night. I had been really shaken by the experience. I felt powerless, angry and really scared. It had all happened so fast. I was in shock and could only stare in horror.

The next morning Richard and I had to go down to the police station where the detective in charge of the case interviewed me. Richard was by my side to vouch for my character. I now found myself assisting the police in their enquiries and wondered if I had become a suspect. I tried to keep my responses calm. But I was released later.

The four young men were captured and at Southwark Crown Court were found guilty of murder after a two-week trial. Each was jailed for life and told they must serve at least twenty-five years before being considered for release. These were evil people already known to the police. Sentencing them, the judge said. "He may have been a target because he was Afro-Caribbean and for no other reason. He had done nothing to these defendants to incur or justify such cruelty. It seems that what led to his death was the colour of his skin. It was a racist murder." At the Shelter, Len branded Jim's murderers as animals.

"That's an insult to the animal kingdom," I said.

It took me some time to regain my composure. I was startled to see how fragile life really was and how cruel man can be to his fellow man. The flick of a knife and Jim's life was snuffed out, his warm blood trickling across the cold paving stones. This reminded me too fully of my own mortality. My time on the streets had taught me about the vulnerability of these people.

Human beings, I discovered, are capable of the most brutal things. Suddenly I felt an intense rage the likes of which I had never experienced before. They had murdered an innocent man in cold blood, a dear gentle man who had never hurt anyone.

That was the most frightening night of my life.

Chapter 27

Everything was all too much for Len. "What's the world coming to?" was his first greeting of the day.

"You tell me," I said.

"A whole lot in the papers about ASBOS. There is a war raging on this new type of thuggery. It was absolutely repulsive. An old lady was abused and had a bucket of manure poured over her head. At another house nails were placed under the wheels of the car in the driveway. We hear of tyres slashed, dead animals left on doorsteps. There are hundreds of incidents of harassment and intimidation in certain parts of the country during the past year," he went on and on.

"Grown up men reduced to tears as property prices soar to new heights. A gang of teenage hoodies. A hard core of local criminals. Something as evil as crime fiction. Some of these young people were handed an anti-social behaviour order. ASBOS were meant to control out-of control-kids and proper order too."

"Radios blasting out of open windows across the street. To be honest ASBOS have little effect. Innocent people are caught in the crossfire. Life is galling for taxpayers. Long suffering, stressed out, spied-on sleep-deprived residents. Beloved plants and trees hacked away."

"You may never know why they choose to behave in such a barbaric way, in this deeply anti-social fashion. Causing mental torture to innocent people. Dog mess smeared on knobs and handles. Cars sprayed or dabbed with paint. Constant harassment. Hanging around in the darkest hours, instilling fear into the residents, threatening people with gardening shears and then stabbing them into van tyres. Going to shoot their actions and take pictures. Happy slappy, they call it."

"There are too many weird programmes on TV or too many violent computer games." Sr. Gabriel listened in to some of the litany of youth crime. "And where do you think it will all end?"

"They think a new 'super ASBO' could tighten the screws on gangland bosses who believe they're above the law. SCPOs Serious Crime Prevention Orders would also make criminals think twice before taking part in Underworld activities. Like ASBOS, SCPOs would ban people from certain activities and could be challenged only in the Court of Appeal."

"Known criminals would have their movements restricted, or be allowed to make only approved phone calls. The aim is to thwart those involved in drug trafficking, immigration crime, money laundering and credit card and identity fraud."

"But doesn't every generation say the same. It wasn't like this in the old days."

"You can be sure of that. It certainly wasn't like that in my youth. We got the cane in school and if I told my old man I would get another wallop. We wouldn't dare commit all these horrendous crimes."

"And would you believe it? Now police have been told to go softly on thugs who breach their ASBO. Not to give them anything more than a warning. Officially anyone under eighteen who breaches an ASBOS, can be locked up for a year but apparently the Home Office has quietly sent a circular to police and prosecutors telling them normally to issue a final warning instead. This revelation makes a mockery of the whole system. Prisons are overflowing. The juvenile prison estate reaches bursting point, so they are desperately trying to find ways of not putting young criminals behind bars. They have tried to think of a means of banning thugs from town centres or housing estates where they have been causing trouble? ASBOS were intended as a weapon in the fight against anti-social behaviour but only if they are properly enforced. But these new suggestions reduce them to nothing more than a gimmick."

It was a dismal, depressing morning and I felt a bit guilty about moving into a corner on my own. I needed to get out. Only my daily routine kept me going. I lived for the moments with Kate and one day quite out of the blue she rushed up to me and said,

"I want you to meet my parents. They have invited you out for a meal. I have to let them know if you are coming so that they can make a reservation at their favourite restaurant."

"I'd love too, and as you know any evening would suit me. My diary isn't exactly full up," I laughed. And I knew I would have to spruce myself up a bit. The next day Kate told me it had all been arranged for the following Friday evening.

"Where am I going," I asked out of curiosity.

"Ah you will have to wait and see."

But when I was getting dressed on the night I had severe reservations. I had never been nervous before about meeting people but this was different. It could be the beginning of the rest of his life.

"We will pick you up from Richard's," Kate said. "I know that is where you will be getting dressed."

The doorbell rang and Kate stood with her parents.

"Hello Kevin. I'm Hilary, Kate's mother." She embraced me and gave me a gentle kiss on the cheek. "We were so pleased you agreed to meet us."

"Thank you so much for your invitation. I have been really looking forward to it." I hoped I wasn't blushing. This was such a special occasion and I had been looking forward to it for quite some time.

Then her Dad stepped forward. "Nice to meet you Kevin! I'm Paul." he held my hand warmly.

"It's only a short walk," Paul said and led the way down towards the Houses of Parliament. We went down a side street and entered the Club where they were members. This was a new venue for me and I was amazed by the building. I couldn't believe that I had lived only a stones-throw from here for nearly two years.

"How amazing," I gasped as I walked into the foyer and looked at the grand stairwell. "This must be the most magnificent stairwell in the world," I said.

"Well yes it must certainly be one of the most beautiful," Hilary agreed.

"Let's eat, shall we?"

"Good idea," Hilary said and Paul led the way up the stairs, through the enormous library with huge portraits of former politicians and into the bar. Paul took our drinks orders and we walked out onto the terrace overlooking the Thames with the London Eye at the other side of the river.

"This must be the most splendid terrace in London," I said. "An excellent venue! I didn't know this place even existed. It is such an honour to be your guests in this magnificent place."

"Our pleasure," Hilary said. I was amazed at how relaxed I felt and how comfortable I was with Kate's parents. All my former apprehension had disappeared. After our drinks we went through to the dining room and were shown to our table overlooking the river. Paul beckoned to the nearest waiter and we were handed leather-bound menus. "The Chateaubriand Vert Pré is definitely worth a try," Paul said.

"Yes, I think I will try it," I said looking across at Kate. "That's something I haven't had before." Kate had said very little all evening. She just sat there smiling at my reactions and allowing me to become acquainted with her parents.

As we ate our meal Paul chatted mainly about the benefits of the club.

"This place was founded in 1882," he explained. "The members and their guests can enjoy the very best service and hospitality. The food is by far the best of any club, and the Head Chef is rated the best in London's gentlemen's clubs."

Hilary had been the perfect hostess all evening and joined in the conversation, "The overall decor is late-Victorian," she said, making this one of the larger and more elaborate clubs to dine in."

I sat enthralled by these affluent surroundings. The dining room was an amazing oak-panelled relic lined with pictures and busts of politicians. The bar and smoking room looked stunning and the terrace had been a perfect setting for drinks before our meal.

"The club's impressive neo-gothic building over the Embankment of the river Thames is one of the largest clubhouses ever built, and was not completed until 1887," Paul explained.

We talked and laughed over the meal and finished the evening with more drinks on the terrace.

"I've had the time of my life." I said when it was time to leave.

"And surely that is a cue for a song tomorrow evening." Kate laughed.

They walked me back to Richard's apartment where we said our goodnights.

"I can't thank you enough," I said as Hilary embraced me. "And I will definitely reciprocate."

"It's alright," Kate said. "All in good time."

"Why didn't you invite them in?" Richard seemed quite disappointed. "I was dying to meet them."

"Don't worry," I said. "I think you will be seeing lots of them in the future.

"Aha, so the evening was successful," Richard said as he handed me a brandy.

"You could say that." I raised my glass.

Chapter 28

"I will make this up to you one day," I told Richard.

"Yes when you're rich and famous and I'm still stuck here in this dump."

"It's certainly not a dump. It has been my refuge."

"My problem is I am powerless to help those other people. My own life is in shreds and I have nothing to offer them."

"I told you, there is nothing in the world you can do."

"By the way," I hesitated. "I need to make a confession. Yesterday I came for my guitar. I made myself a cup of coffee and switched on the TV. Suddenly I was at home and began to realise what an idiot I am."

"Surely that's a step in the right direction. You wouldn't have done that six months ago. You know I have always told you to make yourself at home when you come round. Do you think it has anything to do with Kate?"

"To be honest I think it might have something to do with Kate." I sat deep in thought. My mind was miles away.

We talked about when we were kids, when Richard and I used to ride our bikes down to the village and about all the antics we used to get up to and the serious things in our lives. "Father's death still flashes before me," I said. "A long black limousine, mother leaning on my arm. I phone mother as often as I can. She wants me to come home."

"And that won't be long now," Richard brought down some old photo albums and we looked at the holiday snaps. The man in shorts was my dad. He looked so different when we were on holiday. And there we were in the swimming pool in Tenerife. "They were such happy days," I said, but my mind kept straying back to Monika.

"There is still no news about Monika," I reminded Richard.

"We may never know but you can't blame yourself."

The next morning, on my way to the Shelter, I walked past the station.

I stood in a daze, stunned by the headline in the Metro. I was frightened now. My hands were shaking. I stuck them in my pockets to steady myself.

"Body of a young girl found washed up on the riverbank."

I read on, "The body was still unidentified and we call on anyone who may think they recognise the photo-fit to come forward." I couldn't help myself feeling a sense of panic. Sara had reported Monika as a missing person. I wondered if she had heard the news. She would identify the body. I would ask if I could go with her to help identify the body, or at least satisfy myself that this was not Monika. I was hit by a wave of nausea. The body would be subjected to a forensic examination at the Institute for Forensic Medicine.

Richard advised me to go ahead. I phoned Sara and together we went down to identify the body. The mortuary was cold. I gave a shudder. The attendant folded down the cloth which covered the face. We stood in shocked horror at the white face and blue marks around her neck. It appeared to be death by strangulation.

"Yes I knew this girl," Sarah said. She spent a long time back at the station filling in as many details as she could.

As I walked back under the dim street lights I was still in a state of disbelief. The rain was coming down hard, running in turrets down the footpath and I was now soaked through. I ran under a tree for cover but the rain continued pelting me. It was already dark when the rain eased off and I walked down a side street. A girl dived into a porch illuminated by a row of red lights and entered. Another unlucky prostitute.

Back in the Shelter the next morning, it was as though Monika had never existed.

"You want to know the latest?" Len asked. This morning's debate was about the new waves of crime which were being invented all the time.

"Youngsters in teenage chatrooms," Len said, "left to the mercy of sinister predators. They flock to chat to each other across cities, across continents. But they need to be warned that paedophiles are out there in vast numbers grooming the naïve for under-age sex. These Websites have millions of members. These young people are living out a fantasy life, trying to realise all their dreams. They can make themselves appear as attractive or any shape they like in order to meet those of the opposite sex. This in turn offers them a fantasy world, gives children scope to experiment with their identity."

"In my day, you hung around on the fringes of the dance floor or at local hops waiting for some youth to ask you out. So how at risk are our children nowadays? It is a brave new world of high-tech systems available to the most naïve".

"But in some ways the chatrooms have their own safeguard," I pointed out. "Provided they don't exchange their addresses or phone numbers with a stranger."

"There are other ways to meet friends at clubs or shopping centres," Len said. "In a safe environment where there are other people about."

"We need to be protective but not over-protective," I said. "Parents must be vigilant and cautious, remain watchful if their children are too long on the web. But there is no need for panic. They can and do learn for themselves. It is remote. The person they chat with is not there in the flesh. He is not hiding in the shadows on the way to the bus stop. He is perhaps living out a fantasy of his own."

"But young people can be led astray by the sick and depraved," Len said.

"But they can be led astray regardless of the internet," I reminded him.

"Today a young girl was found hanged with her school tie in her bedroom," Len found another piece of depressing news. "She may have been visiting suicide chat rooms on the Internet," police said. She had become obsessed after a school friend killed himself also using a tie. "Children are given advice online on how to kill themselves. We old folks have no idea of what information is out there, rolling into the children's bedrooms, and into their innocent minds. Very tragic things can happen to these kids. It is chilling to think of it."

Monika's investigation revealed to some extent the numbers involved in human trafficking, a new form of slavery, sensitising people to the problems of human trafficking across international boundaries. Annually more than half of these victims are children, often exploited for sexual purposes including prostitution, pornography and sex tourism. They are also exploited for forced labour including domestic work and factory work. There is a need to propose concrete action and formulate strategies to fight this hideous crime against humanity, to end this hideous crime of modern-day slavery the government should be forced to step up action. Not enough is being done."

Big Ben struck eight and I was still staring at a damp grey sky, with haunted nightmares in my head and every nerve fraught with unknown terror. There was such violence and perversity that it couldn't be captured in words. The clouds had gone, sunset and night were upon me. Then the night was black. I was too restless to sleep. At midnight I got up and pulled the anorak over my head.

As I crossed the bridge, I passed a strange man with a baseball cap covering his face and a cigarette dangling from his left hand. For some unknown reason this person gave me a creepy, disturbing feeling.

Chapter 29

Bonnie and Giles, a young white couple had joined the cardboard but had entered in the most unusual way, swinging from the lampposts in the early glow of dawn. Big Ben had just struck five. I leapt up wondering what on earth was going on. Was it another attack?

"Hello, I'm Giles and this is Bonnie."

"More like Bonnie and Clyde," the girl giggled under her breath. They would certainly bring a new dimension to the cardboard, a little light relief.

The man was about nineteen years old with a rather handsome square face, brown eyes, with a light brown mop of hair and dark complexion, wearing a bomber jacket, jeans and basketball boots. The girl had bleached matted hair, tall and skinny with an enormous tattoo on her arm. She was wearing a short sleeved beige safari jacket and a matching linen skirt.

"There's bedlam around the square," Giles pointed back from the way they had come. "We couldn't stay there another minute. Tomorrow morning we'll be off again on our adventures."

Maybe I should tell them about the Shelter but they didn't seem like the homeless people I saw in the cardboard.

After their grand entrance, they kept to themselves, mainly because they were wrapped up in some newly discovered love affair. Occasionally they spoke with me, mainly when they wanted something or wanted some information. They sometimes threw scraps to Tatters but totally avoided anyone who passed through. I got the impression these were not their real names. They giggled when they had first introduced themselves and appeared to make the names up as they went along. Bob and Bess. Joe and Josie but otherwise they seemed harmless.

As I entered the Shelter, Len was already on his soap box.

"What's new? Thefts from motor vehicles have rocketed. Cars stolen right from under people's noses. The only difference is that there were no cars in my young days up in Yorkshire. And it wasn't so easy to steal a horse and cart."

"It sounds a bit like Ireland," Sr. Gabriel chipped in.

"And dramatic increases in sex offences, burglary and car break-ins but you don't want to know about that Sister. Statistics are soaring. Drastic action is needed to boost police morale and public confidence."

"And hey what do you think of this? A sixty-two year old woman has just had a baby. Britain's oldest mum when her contemporaries are heading toward retirement. After fertility treatment and a donor egg. Personally I think IVF for elderly women is a distortion of nature and should be stopped. Turning grannies into mothers suggests that medical science has taken a step too far. Don't they think that it's time to give way to a younger generation to have babies? A sixty-six year old in Romania gave birth to a daughter last year. Where do we draw the line, seventy, eighty? I think that's stretching it. Ethics have now been thrown to the wind. It's a totally irresponsible society? Children should not be treated as goods. Most people feel this has gone a step too far. Just because things are scientifically possible it doesn't mean we should do it."

"But this woman will no doubt be a responsible parent," I said. "And this little baby will be surrounded by love, if blissfully unaware of the furore surrounding his controversial and historic birth."

"No doubt but the mother will be six foot under by the time the little mite is ready for university."

Len went on with his silent reading and I escaped back into the sunshine. This period of my life had taken on a dream-like quality. I tuned up with a deeply moving piece of music.

"I've got sunshine on a cloudy day. When it's cold outside I've got the month of May...."

Kate appeared and stood listening for a while. Then I walked her back to Waterloo. I sat for a few minutes on a bench outside the station and waited for a signal on my mobile to contact my mother. Ever since Dad's funeral I had kept up constant contact with her and she was happy that at least she now had a phone number but she still pestered me for an address and coaxed me to come back home and take up my new life.

"Soon," I always said. "It won't be long now."

Just before I started to dial her number, my phone rang.

"Kevin is that you?" Mother had got in first.

"I don't want to alarm you, but I have had a bit of an accident. Nothing more than a broken leg but it seems I will be laid up in hospital for a while."

"Oh Mother, I'm so sorry. Which hospital?.... I will be up there right away and I will see if Kate can come with me if that's alright with you."

"Yes of course it is alright. I'm so pleased you have started a new relationship. It hasn't been easy for you but I knew you would move on when the time was right. Don't worry about me. I have everything I need and the hospital is in a beautiful location, surrounded by gardens and woodlands. I have a room of my own and there is a block of visitors' accommodation on the same site."

"Sounds great. I will phone you back with the details of our arrival. Bye Mum. Get well. See you soon."

Kate was excited about the journey. We took an early train on the Saturday morning and then got a taxi to the guest rooms. The sister-in-charge spoke gently and led the way to my mother's room.

Mother was propped up in the bed and I gave her a warm hug. "This is Kate," I said.

"So nice to meet you dear," my mother kissed her and held her hand. "Kevin has told me a lot about you and I am so pleased for both of you."

It was a very welcoming hospital in beautiful surroundings.

Mother seemed to have warmed to Kate immediately. She started telling her all about my birth in 1976. "A miracle," my mother said. "An afterthought," Reg called it. We were both in our early-forties. Obviously the gynaecologist was worried about my age and the safety of the baby but he appeared to have all his faculties, as normal as any baby can be." Then she embarrassed me by telling Kate stories about my early childhood and boasting about my achievements. She continued to embarrass me by talking about my first words, precious remarks, school reports which had to be shown to everyone. She boasted about my music and sporting achievements.

"Reg and I worked together in the law firm," she explained. "We had both had been married before but were childless. Then Martin came along and was the joy of our lives. Finally Kevin arrived and our happiness was complete. The rest is history, as they say."

All the memories came flooding back as I thought of my father. I never said goodbye. I held back the tears. But I had such a wonderful relationship with my mother and now she had welcomed Kate with open arms, almost like she was already part of the family.

I thought about my book which I had started planning in my head. I wondered if I would ever finish the book about my life in this changing world, the good that can come from tragedy. I wanted my readers to know and love my favourite spots in London, to walk the millennium mile, to ride the London Eye, see a play in the Globe and to appreciate our great literary heritage, Dicken's London and Blake's little chimney sweeps. But most of all I wanted them to know about Kate and how she rescued me.

"Thanks for coming, Kate." Mother held her in a warm embrace when we were about to leave. "It has been so nice meeting you. You are like the daughter I never had and I know you have been so good for Kevin" Then she turned to me. "I am very proud of you son," But what had mother to be proud of? I didn't much like what I had done. When I looked back on my life the less there seemed for anyone to be proud of.

Chapter 30

I sang songs about the river. I had heard it say that tragedy affects the passion that anyone puts into a song. I play best when I'm in pain and use my music as a release although I still don't feel like I've been completely able to release it all. It had been a bad morning and my depression had reached rock bottom. No matter how many times Richard tried to reassure me, my guilt still clung like a shawl wrapped tightly around me.

"A broken heart tends to be a great source of inspiration," Roy Groves my old music teacher used to say. Playing my music certainly allowed for some processing of these thoughts and emotions and the healing begins.

I began an old song my mother used to like *'How still runs the river, On its journey to the sea, And still beats my heart, When you're far so far away from me.'*

I was in the middle of the song when Kate bounced up towards me. She had obviously been out jogging in a track suit and trainers.

"Hi there! Why do you always sing such sad songs?"

"Maybe it's because I'm sad. You know some of the saddest people are at their most creative, like Pablo Picasso, one of the most dynamic and influential artists of the twentieth century."

"I have heard a lot about his tragic life. In fact, I was telling the children about him last week during an art lesson. I was telling them how he was lonely, unhappy and terribly poor."

"Why is it that some people can drift through life without a care in the world and others like me seem to be haunted by tragedy," I stood looking out across the red sky.

"Anyway, how is it going?" Kate asked.

"Well I'm trying to earn enough money for a ticket to see *'Hamlet'* at the Globe Theatre. Would you like to come?'

"Of course I would love to go but on one condition that I take you for a tour of the Globe beforehand. I have never been there myself. Have you?"

"No, actually. It's something I have always wanted to do and I would enjoy it twice as much going with you." There I had said it. I had made the first move but I wondered if I had embarrassed her.

"Settled then. We must fix a time and date."

After I packed up my guitar, we went across to one of the coffee booths. The conversation flowed naturally. On the surface we were worlds apart but I knew instinctively that Kate and I had something in common although it mustn't look like that to her at the moment. It was the first time I had taken a girl seriously since Helen. But today I didn't want sad memories to cloud this wonderful new relationship if I dare call it that. It was as if all my dreams had come true in a single instant. My mind was soaring up to the London Eye, above the clouds and down over the golden dome of St. Pauls.

There he was again, the Boston Wanderer, only yards away at another table looking in their direction. Kate ignored his stares. Nothing was going to spoil this moment. Kevin was totally unaware of the stranger behind them.

"Why did she trust me after all she had been through in her previous relationship?" I wondered. For the first time in nearly two years I felt I was a human being again, someone who was wanted, valued for himself, not pitied. I felt I had been cheating both myself and my family and I would soon have to reveal my true identity. Life could not go on like this. The cardboard had to end.

On the following Friday evening, I began to spruce up for the Globe. Richard had said, "Open my wardrobes. Take your pick. And hey, go and get yourself a decent haircut and shave." He placed a £50 note on the table."

"I owe you Richard. One day soon I will pay it all back." He laughed. "I will remind you of that."

My big worry was that someone from the Shelter would see me spruced up for the Globe. Holding Kate's hand as we walked up the south bank, there were many things I wanted to say, important things I wanted to tell her.

"Soon," I thought. "We need to talk," was all I could say right now. Was this the first day of the rest of my life. I couldn't live a lie any longer. Kate told me afterwards that when I went to the bar to get more drinks, there was a hand on her shoulder.

"Still hanging around with that idiot?" She opened her mouth to say something just as I walked back with a tray of drinks. The strange man disappeared behind the nearest pillar.

"Are you alright?" I asked. She didn't want to spoil the evening but felt it was time to say something about the stalking.

"It's that man again."

"He certainly has got the hots for you."

"It's nothing to do with his feelings for me. It's about the horrible things he says about you."

"But he doesn't know me. I expect it's just jealousy. He fancies you and is jealous that you are with me. What does he look like anyway?"

"He is tall and good looking like you," she laughed. "But he has cold staring eyes."

"You're very quiet," Kate said.

"Just thinking. Sorry. Cheers!" I raised my glass and had a sly look around the foyer.

It had been a wonderful evening and I tried to push memories of Kate's stalker to the back of my mind as I walked her back to Waterloo station to catch her train home.

"Thank you for a wonderful evening," I said and kissed her gently on the cheek.

"I should be thanking you. The play was fantastic. Thanks for everything." I watched until she had disappeared at the top of the escalator and then made my way back to Richard's apartment.

I told him I had concerns about Kate's safety.

"London is full of weirdoes but Kate knows that and can look after herself," he said. "And you just keep your head down. You'll be moving out soon but why don't you stay here with me until you make some decisions. The guest room isn't much, but it's got to be better than where you are at the moment. Don't let that idiot worry you."

"I think I will take you up on that offer to move in here, for Kate's sake as well as my own. She is already out of her mind with worry with all these strange people wandering in and out of the cardboard, Jim's murder and the attack on my life have really unnerved her."

"Wise move. It's all yours. At least it leaves you temporarily free of all the uncertainties that surround you out there."

Someone had been stalking Kevin, the familiar figure with hair the colour of embers in the long dark coat he wore in the evenings, flopping like wings around his shoulders, tall, slim and quick. He could be seen lurking in a triangle under a single lamplight, flashing his long fingertips like he was playing a piano, or plucking a guitar. He just stood and stared. There was something strange about him. Something unfathomable.

Chapter 31

Richard said, "You were planning to leave anyway. "Just stay cool. Lie low for a few days until you have made your plans."

"But it has made me completely unnerved and I already have a plan of action worked out." My voice began to sound relieved. Then we went on to talk about Monika's death.

'Unfortunately two more deaths in a big city. 'I know they were your friends, Jock and Monika. I know you had tried to look out for them but such is life in the heart of every big city, in any society," Richard tried to be realistic. "I know how you feel but as they say "Time is a great healer."

"But time won't bring any of them back. My father, Helen, Jock, Monika...."

I knew Richard was right and he did care. He was trying to help me see these tragedies in perspective but as far as I was concerned a human life is a human life to be afforded the dignity we would want for ourselves. I wasn't sure what Father would have thought. The voice of authority was ringing in my ears.

"Move on son! You have you own life to live. You shouldn't have been there in the first place."

And Mother? She would have wrapped her arms around me and said, "I love you son. I know what you are going through. We are always here for you." Mother was a voice for the oppressed. I remembered how many victims, in the course of her career as an Equal Rights lawyer, she had defended against a cruel world of prejudice and sometimes injustices.

I phoned her as often as I could and spoke to her in my heart. "I love you mother. I know you have forgiven me but I can hear you say there was nothing to forgive. I have forgiven myself and I have found the greatest treasure." I told her all about Kate and my feelings for her. "Thank you mother for all the love you have given me and the compassion you have taught me." My mind went back to my parents' tastes in music and I suddenly realised I had inherited music from both of them, the classical and the sentimental. Yes, father had his good points. I remembered how he had sat with me for hours, encouraging me when I was memorising my Beethoven and Vivaldi. I realised how music had been my great therapy during the past two years.

"To create a future, sometimes you had to forget the past, or bits of it," Richard was still speaking."

I knew I couldn't forget but had learned to forgive myself. Kate had given me the courage and the opportunity to come back to the life I loved. But I wouldn't forget my life on the streets and in the Shelter. I would work there with Kate one day but she told me the rules were, I had to live in my own accommodation for at least two years. There were other things I could do in the meantime.

Maura and Richard had taught me to listen all over again and I remembered how I used to feel rejection, failure and pain. Only I myself held the key in my hand to a bright new future. For quite a while negativity had sprouted forth from my own guilt. I had lost faith in my own being but I had now reached an awareness that the only place is here and now. I must switch off the negative feelings of guilt in my head. I could never escape my past, but I knew I had to change to make a better future.

I had learned to forgive myself, to open my heart to forgiveness. I was amazed by the sense of calm now enveloping me. This forgiveness was the first step of regaining control of my life. I had been crippled by the past and this kept holding me back. I had sabotaged my own life, but the real issues that haunted my daily life were now behind me. I pondered on the fact that a lot people put on a mask to hide their real self. Most people make mistakes but only they themselves can stretch their own horizons by allowing themselves to lift the clouds from their minds. Maura had told me once, "Your life is yours alone. Let go of the past once and for all. Live with yourself and for yourself."

Richard had been wrapped in his own thoughts, thoughts of life in general. He felt he had a lot to learn from me. But I was the one who had now come down to earth.

"Yes Richard, you are right. I have to move on."

My goodbyes at the Shelter were not easy.

"Goodbye Kevin and God bless you." Maura put her arms around me. "Don't forget to come back to visit."

"You can be sure of it. I will arrange something very soon," I told her.

I could see her eyes were filling up with tears so I went quickly. In the dining room, I quietly thanked the staff and voluntary workers and told them I would return one day. I waved to everyone and Sr. Gabriel held me in a warm embrace. "God Bless you Kev." she said. "I know what has been going on," she said with a twinkle in her eye.

"I'll be seeing you Sister," I said and gave one last wave as I walked out the door.

Chapter 32

I had now rented my own apartment next door to Richard and had my own money. The first time I went to the bank, I blinked and had to look twice at the staggering amount in my account. The guilt hit me all over again. Here I had been living on the charity of strangers but now I knew I would have to make a donation to the Shelter for my keep during those horrendous months.

"The time has come to reciprocate your parents' kindness," I said to Kate. A date and time was fixed and I had planned to take them to a restaurant in Surrey which Richard had recommended. Reservations were made and I borrowed Richard's car and we set off one Sunday afternoon. It felt strange to be behind the wheel again and I had second thoughts about the car but Richard reassured me.

"You'll be fine," he said. "Just take it easy and let Paul be your navigator."

Being a bit over-cautious, it took me over an hour to reach our destination.

As we pulled into the driveway, I got my first glimpse of the restaurant. It was set in the most tranquil surroundings looking over areas of unspoiled countryside.

"It's stunning," Kate said. "Never before have I been is such an exotic place."

The anxieties of London were miles away. I finally knew Kate loved me and she knew that I loved her.

"I think you will like it...."

But before I could say any more, we were welcomed into a wide foyer where a young girl in a smart black and white uniform beckoned us through and led us up a small flight of steps towards the dining room where we were met by a tall, smartly dressed waiter. The table was covered with a crisp white linen tablecloth with a spray of flowers as a centrepiece. The waiter pulled out my chair and as I sat down, he placed the napkin on my lap. Kate sat opposite me with a warm smile. "It's stunning," she said when the waiter had left.

We had hardly settled in our seats before a wine-waiter came to take our orders. I decided to try one of their red wines but let Paul make the choice. "A small glass of wine for me, I'm driving," I said, "and some iced water."

Then the waiter passed us menus and Kate seemed quite impressed with my confidence in choosing the different courses.

"You know a lot about food," she smiled at me across the table.

"A little," I said.

The conversation was easy. We were all relaxed and everyone was able to speak freely. Kate's parents had become great friends and had always been good listeners.

"I thank you for giving me my freedom," I said to Kate.

She leaned over and touched my hand lightly. "Yours has been a life of courage and I know you have suffered unbearable trials...." she paused.

"We admire your courage," Paul said.

"But I wouldn't be here if it hadn't been for Kate," I said.

After the meal, I dropped a tip on the table. I had now seen life from both sides and appreciated how some people had to struggle on lower wages. As we walked out into the spring sunshine, before getting back in the car, we stood by the side of a pond in the grounds, looked at the fountains and watched the swans glide by.

Kate always seemed to be able to read my thoughts, "It's a new beginning, a turn in the road, a path into another life. Good luck. But remember you're not alone."

"Good luck to all of us," I said. "It's been a wonderful afternoon."

"And thank you Kevin for the fantastic meal," Paul said.

When we got back home I invited them into my new place for coffee. We met Richard in the entrance.

"Back all in one piece," he said.

I laughed. "I hope the car is none-the-worse for the wear. And thanks for the recommendation. We must all do it together one day."

As they were about to leave, Hilary threw her armed around me and kissed me on both cheeks. "Thank you for the journey, for all your help and for the meal. The food was delicious." Paul took my hand and patted me on the shoulder.

"See you," we waved each other goodbye.

Kate stayed back and we went for a stroll along the south bank of the river. We had a lot to talk about.

Chapter 33

2006 was a mammoth year in my life. It was the year of my liberation, the year of the Queen's eightieth birthday and the year when everyone was talking about the FIFA World Cup. For me it was a year of new life but the greatest of all it was the year I developed my relationship with Kate.

It was a big day in London on the Queen's eightieth birthday. Kate and I walked along the streets which were already lined with people waving flags. As we turned the corner into Trafalgar Square, a beggar sat tucked in a doorway trying to avoid being squashed by the crowds. I stepped over and put some money in his dirty cap and an excited smile lit up his face.

"God Bless you sir," he said looking up at me with gratitude in his eyes and I think I saw a tear running down the aged, withered face. There was an air of excitement around. Everyone had looked forward to this day. It was a gigantic media event. Reporters and cameramen were everywhere on high pedestals, racing in front of the crowd. The aircraft burst over the grey water and turned round going east, then back again, circling around the city centre. We had arrived in front of Buckingham Palace where the Queen watched from the balcony. People tried to climb trees or on top of fences to get better views. A young woman clutching a little boy by the hand pushed her way in front of us to get a better view. The boy was waving a flag and straining to see the sentries standing motionless in their boxes.

"What an amazing reign!" Kate said. "She witnessed the first space missions, a man walking on the moon," Kate said. "She lived through the war years and periods of other disasters both at home and abroad. The Berlin Wall has been built and razed to the ground all in her lifetime."

It was a great day for the Queen but for me too it was a day to remember as we walked back hand in hand to Waterloo station and as Kate kissed me goodnight, my happiness knew no bounds.

Chapter 34

I strolled along the South Bank towards the National Theatre in a sudden urge, now that I had started, to regain some of his past cultural interests. I had been a keen enthusiast of the National's extensive programme of talks and readings. My father had even taken me on a backstage tour. As a small boy I was lost in the high walls. I still remember the musty smell of rails of costumes and high walls and props. Today I sat in the foyer listening to a jazz pianist taking part in the free foyer music programme. I thumbed my way through the new season's programme.

When Kate took the train home, I was back on my busking patch. The National Theatre had created a new edge on my existence, gave me a new enthusiasm for life.

At this time a song had been sweeping the nation, "*You raise me up*". It became one of my favourites and I found it to be popular with my audience. It was amazing the difference it made to donations by passers-by. It became one of my favourites of all time. I thought of this song as Kate's anthem.

"*You raise me up, so I can stand on mountains; You raise me up, to walk on stormy sea....*"

I imagined the music notes floating up and over the London Eye, far beyond the maddening crowd.

Someone had once said that a singer never reached those heights until they had been broken hearted. I had certainly experienced heartbreak.

"*There is no life ^= no life without its hunger; Each restless heart beats so imperfectly. But when you come and I am filled with wonder, Sometimes I think I glimpse eternity...*"

Chapter 35

I was just relieved to be outside and away from the street that had become my prison. Kate had reached the door before me. Although she was dressed simply, she looked stylish and elegant and as always radiantly beautiful. As she stood in front of me like a supermodel, a vision of beauty in a white silk dress, my heart missed a beat. "You are the best thing that's ever happened to me," I said and reached down to kiss her before ringing the doorbell.

When the door opened a beautiful girl stood there, dark shoulder-length hair and dressed in a simple black dress. "Come in. I'm Louisa. You must be Kevin." She gave me a warm embrace.

"Richard has told me all about you. And then you are Kate, Welcome! Come on in." Richard and Louisa had prepared an amazing meal and as he uncorked the first bottle, Richard said, "Let's drink a toast to Kevin!" They raised their glasses. "To Kevin!"

After the last course had been served, we sat back and relaxed. The conversation was mainly how I had survived after so many setbacks.

"Thank you for bringing me back from the edge of the precipice. I couldn't have done it without you," I said and raised my glass to Richard and Kate.

"You brought yourself back," Richard said.

"Here here," Kate and Louisa agreed and the glasses were raised again.

"Yes but my life over these two years, in all these months, all these weeks, and long endless dark nights had encompassed more than a lifetime of struggle, emotion and pain."

"But you have survived," Richard said. "And I believe it has made you a much stronger person."

"I can assure you I didn't feel strong out there. The ground had gone from under my feet and I had been tumbling into a darkness and a madness, suspended on the very edge of existence. The door to my real self and my real life had horrifyingly slammed shut. But now I have got a glimpse of a future that can eclipse the present, and bring new visions of hope, a future that had once appeared far beyond my present and immediate grasp."

"I think Maura has been an inspiration for you," Kate said.

"Without a doubt, I couldn't have made it without her. A real difference has been made by the intense loyalty and affection shown by my friends, you who have trusted me, remained true, even when others had cast me off. This more than anything helped to restore my sense of belief in myself. So many of the staff at the Shelter were warm and supportive. Every day I saw small acts of genuine empathy and compassion."

I knew that not one day had I been left to rot away alone in this state or to join the ranks of the sad, lonely victims of this cruel conditions who have no one to be there for them. It was like I had stepped off the cliff into the unknown. It seemed quite simply the only way to go. For the rest of my life over the past two years a number of fantastic friends and generous donors who were to improve things for us in an amazing way, but I had not the slightest idea or could even begin to guess how they would touch my life with such kindness and warmth.

"Yes, it's amazing how love can provide the bridge across a sea of pain and loss," Richard said.

"On the way if have met many interesting and wonderful people. Their response to our predicament has been just marvellous. I have experienced so much kindness and genuine warmth."

"It is often the case that being close to adversity brings out the best in people," Richard said.

"Absolutely. It is certainly true to say that the affection and respect I have for all those who have helped me know no bounds."

"And I think it has changed you quite a lot as a person," Richard said.

"One of the greatest changes to me deep down in best described as feeling everything with a greater intensity. I saw with horror what all the others had to endure day after day. Life presented itself as a vision of all that is monstrous, unfair and inhuman. The nights were particularly horrendous. There was no way of knowing what each night would bring. Any night could be the abrupt beginning of a crisis and I might not reach the morning. There are so many things to adjust to. There are no words to describe how you have all helped get me back on track, which to be honest, I couldn't have anticipated in my wildest dreams. To sum it up, I think I found out what it is to be human."

We then went on and talked a lot about Richard's work and how he had met Louisa.

"We applied for a junior partner and after over a hundred applicants, we shortlisted five. Louisa was one of them. The rest, as they say, is history."

I proposed a toast to Richard and Louisa. Glasses were raised once more, "To Richard and Louisa."

But Richard wanted to get back on my story of survival. "Do you think this whole experience has changed you in any way and what were the things you missed most?" he asked.

"Of course one of the toughest things that I really did miss was the stimulation and challenge of work. Although my job had been stressful and exhausting at times, I enjoyed the professionalism and warmth of so many of my colleagues, especially the many laughs we had together."

"Let's drink to work," Richard went around replenishing the glasses.

"This reminds me of a visit to Tbilisi and the amazing hospitality of our hosts," I said. "They had prepared a banquet for our arrival, about twenty of us round the table and at regular intervals people proposed toasts to one thing or another. This went on until the early hours and as the drinks flowed generously, we became more and more inebriated and high-spirited. Then the singing and dancing began, the men dancing with each other in some crazy Cossack style. The women by then sat on the sofas exhausted and we were barely able to drag ourselves off to bed. But we had to pay the price the following morning and were offered the antidote, a hangover soup."

"By the way did you ever find your luggage that time?" Richard asked. "I remember your postcard '*Here in Tbilisi but my toothbrush is still in Amsterdam.*'

"Eventually! But not until the day before we left. But that is another story."

It was an incredible feeling to have returned to the world of the living, amongst friends enjoying good food and good company. I realised that I was finally taking some control over my life again. I was a completely different person from the one who had left two years before.

"It's hard to believe that the time had finally come for my release," I said. "Even harder to believe, though that this is me. I am grateful that I can at least start to reconstruct a vestige of what it was to live like a real person again. It feels like the most enormous triumph over fate. It has become an imperative to restore my old existence.

"It truly has been a love story and one that has developed and survived against all the odds. You bring out the best in him Kate," Richard raised his glass again.

After dinner I sat alone gently strumming my guitar and singing softly, more to myself. I was pondering each line of a song, which in many ways made sense of my own life but also helped me to remember that there are great mysteries which we will never fully comprehend. I sang slowly and from the heart and by now I had an audience. Apparently Louisa had heard all about my singing.

"Come on Kevin, give us a tune," Kate and Richard sat contentedly on the settee listening and sipping their Martinis and like myself drinking in the words of the song.

"I've looked at life from both sides now...."

The Joni Mitchell song had helped me reflect on my own life. Just when I thought I had my life sorted and my career well underway, tragedy had struck. I now had a totally different perspective on tragedy, on homelessness and on human nature and my two years on the streets had given me the opportunity to see the many-faceted sides of human nature. There is the warm, tender caring element, but the shadows of anger, rejection and guilt that can lurk within our beings.

When I looked at life from both sides I had allowed myself to mature and grow from having experienced the joyful as well as the painful experiences and emotions. I realised we have to see the light and shade and like a good painting life has its sunshine and shadows, but we have to live life balancing the give and take, ups and downs, joys and pains always with a need to compromise. I reflected on my own human drama, which had given me time to observe, to learn from our interactions and choices. I was now full of the awe and wonder of life. But I knew that complacency is a dangerous thing and has caused many falls. I must go on learning but Kate and I would work things out together.

"Hi there Kev, are you still with us?" This time it was Kate reminding me that the song had finished ages ago.

"Just one more," Louisa pleaded. I caught just a glimpse of the Eye from the side window of Richard's apartment. "Life revolves like the Eye, like a windmill," I thought. A Dusty Springfield song, 'The Windmills of my Mind' seemed to sum up my mood which matched the words of the song, *"Like a circle in a spiral, Like a wheel within a wheel...."*

When I had finished Kate asked, "How about another song?"

'Or a walk along the river?' I suggested.

We all agreed that a walk would be good. We needed some fresh air and some exercise. I was so pleased that Richard had found the same happiness that I had found. "Well you've been out of touch with the world so long, it must be difficult to know what to believe," Richard said.

"On the contrary I am the one who had been in touch with the world," I laughed.

We chatted as we walked along the South Bank.

"Do you still play bridge, as a matter of interest?" Richard asked.

"Yes but very badly, I haven't touched a pack of cards for years.

"And you?" Richard looked at Kate.

"Yes a little," she said.

"That settles it. We all play a little so what about a bridge supper next week?"

It was agreed but Richard might live to regret this bright idea.

As they strolled back, what they didn't know was that they were being watched by the shadow on the bridge, that mysterious being standing in the shadows.

Chapter 36

After supper, over a final glass of wine, we sat chatting about our younger days when Richard reminded me of the time we learned to play bridge in the sixth form.

"Remember the chaplain, the Rev. Browning. He used to call his mistakes '*clerical errors.*'"

"And when he did well we accused him of '*divine intervention*'," I said.

"And Colin and Jean. I wonder what happened to them."

"They got married I believe, still playing bridge and I guess driving everyone crazy. And Gerry's aggression! Remember Gerry, head of foreign languages? I was pleased not to be in one of his classes. He terrorised the students," I recalled.

"And he terrorised us at the bridge table too. Had to win at all costs. We sat in fear and trepidation when we saw him approaching."

"There were two girls who were always arguing and those over-bearing school prefects, who tried to dominate everyone in the club. I'm surprised we ever learned anything."

"Those were the days," Richard said. "But now down to business." Richard set up the card table. He took out the bidding boxes and two packs of cards from the glass cabinet and started to shuffle. Louisa shuffled the spare pack of cards and then put them on her right hand side. "They have a little ditty at the Monday club," she said.

"If you're not demented quite, put your cards upon the right." Everyone looked up. "Where did that come from?" Richard asked.

"You know those elderly ladies at my Monday club. They have the strangest rules. Some of them have been playing bridge for about a hundred years. Good players, but this one makes sense.

If I put my cards on my right, then we know it's the person on my right who is the next dealer."

"Fair enough," Richard said, "but we play duplicate at our club with set boards."

Then we were off, counting cards and honour points. Richard decided to keep a score sheet. The bidding was off to a good start. Kate and I played in partnership. We bid and comfortably won our first contract in four spades. After walking away with the first four games, I said, "I think our partnership is coming along quite nicely," and Kate looked across with a mischievous twinkle in her eye.

Poor Richard. You could see his frustrations mounting. They were beginning to flounder. I doubled for take-out and Kate responded. It was plain-sailing after that. Kate and I were stronger players, grabbing and winning all the contracts. In the next game, I had three inescapable losers in diamonds. When the dummy went down I saw that I would have to hold fire on drawing trumps and dispose of his diamond losers first. After I had discarded all three of my diamond losers the game was ours. I led the last master club and claimed the contract. "The rest are good," I said laying down my hand.

"Well played," Richard looked across with a look of defeat on his face.

A few deals later I found himself in 3NT. My face lit up when Kate put down the dummy. "Wonderful. Thank you partner." I held up twice in spades to break communications between the defenders' hands. Finally I flipped the remaining cards on the table, "They're all good," I said. "Another 600 for you." Richard wrote on the score sheet. Kate and I were already over a thousand points ahead.

"Your partnership seems to be progressing very nicely," Richard said when he came back to fill up their glasses. In the next game I make a reverse bid and Kate knew exactly what my bid meant and raised it to game. Then the big one. Kate leapt to the six-level over my 4NT bid.

In the next game Kate made a jump bid and after assessing our two hands, a gleam came into her eyes. I knew a slam was on but decided to take my time and go slowly on the bidding. Going down the Blackwood route I was pleasantly surprised to discover that we had all the aces and kings so I jumped straight to a grand slam. Kate would be playing it but I had every confidence in her skills. "Another 2220 points," Richard smiled but you could see the desperation in his eyes.

Then I dealt myself a Yarborough. "Oops, I thought," and when Kate passed I was relieved in a way. It would give Richard and Louisa a chance to score. . It turned out that Kate had three high card points. Richard started to play badly. He and Louisa exchanged glances. Louisa drew the last trump and claimed the contract. Kevin breathed a sigh of relief. Finally they had a positive score but two or three rounds later, Kate and I were still wiping the floor with them and I began to feel a bit uncomfortable.

Then the real disaster struck. They had agreed on a fit in hearts and Richard went down the Blackwood route to a slam. After his 4NT bid, Louisa sat with a look of incomprehension on her face. She thought for a while, fumbled a bit with the bidding box and finally passed. Richard just sat there helplessly. I felt a bit mean but bid the double. I had two aces and two kings so should be able to take them down. But now Richard was stuck in 4NT with a void and a singleton in his hand. When the dummy went down he saw that he could have comfortably made a grand slam in hearts. "Oh dear," you could hear inward sighs around the table. I felt a bit mean but intended to take full advantage of the situation and once more robbed poor Richard of his contract.

Next time Richard and Louisa ended in a four-heart contract. But they would soon regret it. "Double," I said in an apologetic tone. Richard raised his eyes to the ceiling, as the 3-point dummy appeared on the table. "Another one bites the dust," he thought.

Another unconvincing auction left Richard and Louisa in a 4-spades contract and Richard maintained a neutral expression, not wishing to trigger a reaction from the opposition. They had only played six games but it seemed like an eternity to Richard. "Oh dear," I thought. "Bad split. Unlucky," Kate tried to make excuses for them too. Four spades doubled and down went the dummy. "Oh dear, another disaster." Richard's sole aim was survival but that was quite out of his reach. It was all becoming too much for Louisa. A subsequent unsuccessful heart finesse and the game went down.

"The problem was in my bidding. Louisa apologised again.

"Interesting hand," Richard said. He decided to take control of the auction but it was too late. He looked blankly at the dummy. "Such good defence you made there," Richard did his best to be polite. Richard was dummy. When he put down his hand he decided to go off and fill up the glasses. When the dummy went down Richard's face dropped. Louisa had three points and only three spades. "Another one for the slaughter," I thought. Richard gave a wry smile across at Louisa. Louisa's bid was misleading. It wasn't so much that she was a bad player, but the high standard of play at the table was making her nervous. Then Richard did well on a part-score. But they should have been in game and got a measly 120 points instead of a top of 620. The situation couldn't be worse.

I was beginning to regret the idea of an after-dinner bridge game and felt the need to do something to restore the situation.

"Shall we swap partners after the next game?" I suggested, hoping to spare them any more embarrassment. "It's not as though we're playing in some important world championship," I said.

"Good idea." Everyone agreed.

"And until we get used to playing together, I think it's a good idea to discuss the bidding as we go along just to make the play a bit more informal and relaxed.

It wasn't long before the scores were reversed and I saw that Richard and Kate were a couple of hundred points ahead. They were just cruising along.

Then I bid 2-clubs. Louisa sat with a puzzled expression on her face, thought for a bit and then passed.

"Is it alright if I explain?" I asked the table. "Go ahead," they agreed.

"I'm not telling you I like clubs," I told Louisa.

"Ah, yes. I remember now. You have a strong hand, 23+ points."

She was finally seeing the light. They gave her permission to take back her bid and the game progressed as normal and ended up in 4 spades which Louisa made with an overtrick.

In the next game I knew she could make all thirteen ticks but decided to leave it in a small slam. She did make all thirteen. "Well done, Louisa. In an instant all traces of nerves vanished from her face.

She was on a run and won the next two games. "Well played Louisa, Top score again." She was well pleased with her play now. She took the first eight tricks and another two trump tricks which gave her the contract. Richard and Kate were powerless to take her down.

I sat back quietly in my chair. "Well done," I said. We're having our best run ever. I smiled across at Louisa.

In the next game her eyes lit up when she saw my dummy.

She sat back and sipped her wine thoughtfully as she planned her game. Then she was off again.

"Well played indeed," everyone agreed. Against all expectations, it seemed that she was now going to make it. Although her bidding needed some attention, her playing was superb. Louisa's game ended on a note of absolute triumph.

"That's a splendid fire you have made for us but it does tend to make us quite thirsty," I laughed.

I helped Richard take the table down and put the cards back in the glass cabinet.

The conversation turned to anything and everything. We were all completely relaxed. I beamed my congratulations to Louisa and the others nodded in agreement. She smiled warmly.

"Shall we retire to a more comfortable seat and have a brandy?" Richard said.

It was history in the making, a foursome was born.

Louisa had baked an oversized Victoria sponge. Not a crumb was left and everyone praised her on her baking skills.

"And her bridge skills," I added and everyone laughed.

Richard said, "We must do it again."

"After I have had a few lessons," Louisa said.

"You were fine," I said. "In fact you are a much better player than I am."

Chapter 37

I had reached a moment of great significance in my life. The moment of decision and high resolve had arrived. A strange calm settled over me and plans were swiftly made. I was acutely aware of the pain and anguish I had caused so many good people.

First, I wrote to Mother. She already had my mobile phone number and the address of my apartment but there were things I could not have told her over the phone. I needed to explain in writing how I had lived my life for the past two years. I told her about Kate, how she had given me the moral support I needed and how she and Maura had treated me with such understanding, when few others would and how they had helped me make my final decision.

I surveyed the events of the past few days and how things needed to move forward. My triumphant mood filled the air. Kate and I went shopping to buy clothes, gifts to take home and supplies for Tatters. We were full of the joys of life.

My solid dependable father had shown me the rights and wrongs of the world and with my gentle mother together they had made a magical combination, the best parents a son could ever have and they had made me the person I had been and hopefully could be again.

"Come on the school outing. We are going to the British Museum," Kate pleaded. "We are always short of men to take charge."

"No, sorry I must turn that down. People still see me as a homeless person. There could be all sorts of speculation and it wouldn't be fair to you."

"Well next time," she said.

"Yes definitely next time."

It had been a whirlwind week. Kate had broken up for the Christmas holiday. After that things moved very fast. Everything was suddenly on the move, the old landmarks of my depression were left far behind. There was so much to catch up on, so many business matters to attend to. But there was a tremendous amount of joy in my life now that Kate was at my side throughout the ordeal of getting my life back into gear. The song *Yellow Ribbon* was running through my mind. *I'm going home, I've done my time.*

"Right," I said, "One of the most urgent tasks is to go car hunting. Would you like to come with me on a visit to the car show rooms?"

"Try and stop me," Kate said.

I now had access to my bank account and money was no longer any obstacle.

Kate's eyes popped out of her head the first time she saw my bank statement. There were no secrets between us now.

"We need our own vehicle as soon as possible and I'm sure you will help me make the right choice." We were already on our way out the door. We went to the nearest car show room and walked around admiring the variety of cars on display. We looked at several makes and models of various ages and specifications. My eyes were fixed on the bright red Ferrari in a large space in the corner. It was cordoned off with thick red velvet-type ropes on brass stands.

"Nothing is too good for us," I thought.

I stood there dreaming about going back home with Kate in the red Ferrari glinting in the sun as it glided over the tiny road on the last part of our journey. The iron gates would swing open at the press of a button as I turned into the driveway and drove through the shade of the trees. In my mind's eye, I rounded a bend and the house slowly came into view. It was my small kingdom hidden from the rest of the world by dense foliage. There were even security cameras tucked away unobtrusively. The house was large enough for a family of at least a dozen but it had been my home with my parents for all those years. I dreamed that Rosemary, my old Nanna had appeared at the front door. It would be a wonderful reunion and before I returned to London I would say my goodbyes, turn on the ignition of my Ferrari and it would hum to life. I could see mother waving goodbye and watching as we disappeared down the driveway, so happy for us.

"No harm in dreaming," I suddenly came back down to earth.

"How about this little Focus," Terry the salesman led us over to a shiny new red Focus.

"A perfect choice," I said. "I had one of those before when I was in college. What do you think Kate?" Kate just stood there with a broad smile. She had seen me standing in a daze admiring the Ferrari.

"Perfect," she gave me that knowing smile and then said, "That way I will be able to share the driving. I thought you were going to go for one of those sophisticated computerised things. They frighten the life out of me. Dad has one and I wouldn't touch it with a barge pole."

So that was that!

"I'll be back tomorrow with the cheque," I told Terry.

It was only a matter of getting my bank to agree. Ironically this account had been put aside in my name by my parents for an emergency. Well this was an emergency although maybe not to Ferrari proportions.

That night I switched on the computer in my bedroom. It had been a moving-in gift from Richard. Everything was in working order even my internet account. I had always maintained my email address from the past. I knew that Mother had received an I-pad for her birthday from her former work colleagues, so we had now moved back into the twenty-first century.

The next day I went to the bank to raise a cheque for the garage. It was signed and sealed. Terry arranged the road tax and allowed me to use the computer in his office and the insurance was instant over the internet. The deal was clinched.

Chapter 38

All our preparations were made and we had fixed the date for our journey to Derbyshire. It was like a pilgrimage into the past and I was filled with fear and excitement, my mind full of mixed emotions as we left London behind and arrived on the motorway.

We didn't talk much. It was a comfortable relationship. Kate knew why I was quiet and just sat enjoying the views. I was almost thirty-one, no job no home.

"Tomorrow is another day," I thought. "A new family and of course Kate, a job, a home and eternal happiness but I couldn't help thinking it might not be as simple as that.

With two stops at service stations along the way to give Tatters a run around, the journey took us nearly three hours. Finally we were almost there but my thoughts were in turmoil, as I slowly rounded the final bend the house was in full view.

Kate gasped. "Is this your house?"

"It's only a house," I said and it was with great trepidation that I drove on up the driveway. Mother was already waiting in the door at the top of the steps, still on one crutch.

It was as though time had stood still and I had never been away and that those awful tragedies had not happened. Kate handed me a tissue to wipe my tears. It was like I was five years old again and my first day at school. Nothing had changed, the house, the lawns were precisely as they had always been.

"I have been dreaming about this moment," Mother said as she gave me an enormous hug.

"Take it easy Mother," I said as she tried to steady herself.

"I thought this day would never come," Mother wouldn't let go of my hand and I could see the tears rolling down her cheeks.

"Oh Mother, how could I do this to you? I promise to make it up to you. You didn't deserve this."

"Come here son," she said. "All that is behind us now. Stop your blathering and let me see Kate." They threw their arms around each other.

"This is a wonderful day. The day I have longed for. Welcome home son. Welcome Kate."

"But there is someone else we want you to meet." I said.

"I'll fetch him," Kate said and I handed her the car keys.

"Who else?" Mother asked. "Is it Richard?"

In a moment Tatters was bounding up the steps, wagging his tail and licking everyone he met.

"Mother, this is your new friend. I wanted it to be a surprise. His name is Tatters."

"Oh my goodness, what a surprise! Come here Tatters." We all hugged again and laughed and cried.

"This is the happiest day of my life," Mother said. "And this little chap has made my day complete. Come here Tatters," she patted him on the head and they already seemed to belong to each other.

Rosemary and James had stayed discreetly in the background but Tatters drew our attention to them. Rosemary had been my childhood Nanny and was housekeeper ever since. Her husband James was our gardener and maintenance man. They lived in the cottage at the foot of the drive and had been such loyal friends over the years. No one could ever replace them in our lives. The cottage was now their own property, left to them in my father's will.

More hugging and kissing and laughing and crying.

"You two have done a great job looking after the old place," I said.

"Remember your family has been paying us for that," Rosemary reminded me.

"But you have always gone over and above the call of duty," I said.

"Come into the kitchen," Rosemary said. "You must be ready for a hot drink."

It was just like old times as Rosemary got everyone seated and I drew my own chair up to the table, in my favourite spot overlooking the herb garden and the path leading down to the river. My father's little boat was still moored at the bottom of the lawn. The fire was glowing in the hearth near where I sat.

"Here you are Kevin," Rosemary handed me a long toasting fork and a plate with large chunks of bread.

"Does this bring back memories?" she asked. "Remember when you used to come home from school and made a bee line for the kitchen?"

"How can I ever forget? You always allowed me to make my own tea and the smell of toast has always reminded me of you."

I sat there in wonderment, toasting fork pointed towards the warm glow of the fire. From where I sat I gazed across the gentle waters of the river Trent, a much smaller, gentler river than what I had been used to in the past two years.

Mother and Kate had already established a relationship. They chatted about London, Kate's family, the journey up the motorway but mostly about Tatters.

"We will have to go down to the pet shop and buy you some basic requirements," Mother patted his head and he wagged his tail in agreement.

"You don't have to worry about that. His bed is in the car and lots of other supplies he will need." Kate said.

Rosemary busied herself with the tea and coffee and she called out to James who was sweeping up leaves on the back patio. "Tea up," she shouted tapping the window with the handle of the knife. I was back in my favourite place from my childhood. Everything had been pieced back together again.

After tea Mother said. "It is time for some welcome-home champagne in the wine bar on the river. We sat out on the narrow heated balcony and this time it was James's turn to do the serving. He seemed to know all about champagne, wines and beers.

There was more laughter now than tears. "Hi Tatters what you think old Jock would think of this place," I asked.

"I think he would be particularly interested in the drinks cabinet," Kate said.

I gazed for a long time across the river where majestic willows dangled their branches in the water. The house had been aptly named "*Willow Brooks*".

When we all felt we had enough to drink Mother said, "Time to take Kate on a guided tour."

The estate was quiet and almost seemed deserted as we wandered back into the main building, through the mosaic patterned floor of the hallway and into the wide gallery which served as a corridor linking the two wings of the house.

"This is the billiards room. It was my father's favourite pastime apart from his Bridge that is but I was never much good at billiards." Then we headed up the wide stairway to the bedrooms. We stood on the large landing overlooking the tennis court with views down a side path leading towards the river, past the kitchen garden and orchard of cherry, plum, apple and pear trees all pruned and put to bed for the winter.

"I think Jock would definitely have liked this one," I said as I led Kate down the spiral stairway to the wine cellar where dusty shelves housed a variety of wines.

"Wow!" Kate said. "I expect some of these are valuable."

"I imagine so. Strangely I had never taken much interest in that sort of thing."

In the evening the table was laid for dinner but first we were shown to our rooms.

"Your bed has been waiting for you. I have changed the sheets regularly. It is always made up just like when you left it. I have never let anyone else use your room. Your aunties and cousins come frequently but your room is sacrosanct.

"Thanks Nanna!" There was so much I had to thank her for.

Back in the dining room, the sun was setting and the room was a haze of pinks and whites. There was a large bowl of mixed flowers in the centre of the table and two candelabra which had been in the family for generations. The place looked immaculate with white linen tablecloths and white serviettes. I suddenly had the feeling that it might always have been like that but I had never paid any attention before. My parents often had colleagues around from work mostly after Martin and I had gone to bed and no doubt Rosemary had always put on this magnificent spread.

I noticed there were five place settings on the table. "Are we expecting visitors?" I asked Mother.

Just then there was a light tap on the door. Richard never rang the doorbell. It was like that when we visited each other, we never stood on ceremony. Richard's house was next door with a small gate leading out onto our back lawn. We had never used the front entrances. There he stood beaming from ear to ear with Louisa on his arm.

"What's all this hilarity?" he asked.

"Oh just browsing through some old photos," Mother said as she got up made room for our visitors.

"Welcome home," Richard said as he took my hand. Kate and Louisa had already embraced each other and I could see we were in for a friendly evening. Mother pressed the small buzzer on the mantelpiece and in a flash James and Rosemary were there tending to our every need. The conversation was relaxed just like old times. Richard had always been like another son and there were no secrets between us.

The conversation flowed easily. We were like one big happy family, open and honest with each other.

"I've often wondered about you Richard," Mother said. "You're single, attractive and successful. You were always working at that law firm and being totally focused on the partnership. You never had time to socialise, too busy finding your feet in this busy modern world. But when you came around yesterday and introduced me to Louisa I was so delighted for you."

"Well I think you are right on one point. I didn't have time to go out looking for romance. Louisa came to me."

"What do you mean?"

He explained about the advertisement for a new junior partner from a hundred applicants and how they had shortlisted five and then selected one person, Louisa!"

"Trust a lawyer to behave like that," I laughed.

"Well what about a layabout pinching one of the Shelter's prettiest young volunteers?" Richard said.

I thought of the strange twists and turns of fate.

"You know that's quite different. It was an even playing field," I said.

"I don't know how on earth you make that out?" Everyone laughed.

The conversation came round to work and future plans.

"You have already been promised a partnership in your uncle's law firm in London, your firm now too of course," Mother told me. I had a lot to learn and a lot more planning to do.

After dinner we moved into the sitting room where James served the port. Kate's eyes scanned the photos on the walls and mantelpiece. I suddenly stood in shocked horror. The instant I saw Martin's picture with that evil glint in his eyes, my pulse began to race. Old fears and recurring nightmares came flooding back.

"Are you alright," Kate asked. She took my hand and steadied me. Just at that instant Rosemary appeared with a tea-tray. Rosemary poured the tea and coffee using a small silver tray. She placed an arm around my shoulders and immediately all the old fears and guilt were gone. She placed a crystal sugar-bowl and matching cream jug in the centre of the table and used the same china tea cups and saucers which had been so carefully guarded over the years.

"A far cry from coffee in a jam jar," I laughed to myself but "This is lovely Nanna," was all I could say. Kate sat smiling and couldn't take her eyes off me and all the beautiful surroundings.

Mother and I sat holding hands. "You must come to London when we get our new house," I said.

"I'll think about it but it would be a big culture shock for me."

"Well why not travel down with us in the car sometime or with Richard. I'm sure Tatters would love to see his old stamping ground again."

"I'll give it some serious thought," she said.

I had regained my equilibrium and minutes later Mother had joined us and we were pouring through large photo albums and laughing at all the fashions over the years.

"Oh my goodness and we thought we looked beautiful in those outfits," Mother burst out laughing.

It was a fine night, a myriad of stars mingling with the rows of footlights up along the sides of the driveway.

We talked and laughed for some time but eventually Richard stood up and we all thanked Rosemary and James for the wonderful meal. Mother went into her little parlour to watch one of her favourite TV shows and we strolled out into the garden and crossed the lawn, until we had reached the two swings.

"Do you remember we used to try and see who could go higher?"

Richard laughed and the air was filled with nostalgia and reminiscences of a bygone age.

"Well it's been a long day for you two," Richard said. "We will just slip away. See you tomorrow."

When they left Kate said, "Yes it's been a long day but I am still too full of excitement to turn in for the night."

"What would you like to do? We could go for a spin on the bikes."

"Fantastic," Kate's eyes lit up with enthusiasm so we decided to get the bicycles out of the garage. James had kept them oiled and in good repair.

We went back indoors to tell mother about our plans and to fetch warm jackets and scarves.

"Good night son. Good night Kate." Mother embraced us both and there were tears of joy in her eyes.

We were in the beautiful foothills of the Pennines. Together we rode down the narrow road winding through the woods with the sun slanting through the tops of the trees, past a farmyard with a barn crammed with yellow corn and the grey-domed manor house in the park. The fields were marked with thick clumps of trees and cattle grazed peacefully.

We stopped briefly to take it all in.

"Such a haven of tranquillity!" Kate said.

Then we moved on beyond the fields, further stretches of woodlands, past the gleam of the silver river, and then more hills rising up. The top of the tower of the village church could be seen among elm trees, a spark of light glittering on the weather vane.

We paused for breath outside the village pub.

"Do you want to go in for a drink before we head back."

"No that would spoil the magic," Kate said.

I knew exactly what she meant and I had never seen this place look so beautiful. It was now over two years since I walked around the village green with Helen. Richard had warned me that going home for the first time could be quite emotional and

I hadn't anticipated how I was feeling at this moment. This had been the most poignant moment since our arrival. I tried to fight back the tears but Kate took my hand. "Are you alright?"

"Yes just a bit taken by the beauty of it all. I don't think I fully appreciated this place before. When my parents decided on this location, they said that it must be the most beautiful village in England."

But Kate knew there was more to it than that and in an instant she had snapped me out of it.

"Right! Let's race each other back home," she said. I couldn't resist that challenge. We jumped on our bikes and off we went back down the track laughing and swerving almost knocking each other into the trees but we soon began to slow down to a steady pace for the final part of the journey.

The moon rose slowly over the world as we cycled back home. There stood the great house with its windows robed in silver. As we went in through the large oak doors, the grandfather clock in the hall struck ten.

Rosemary was out in a shot. She never went to bed until we were all safely gathered in for the night.

"It has indeed been a long day," Kate said suppressing a yawn.

"Come in children and have a hot drink. You must be perished." Rosemary had a way of appearing out of nowhere just when we needed her most. She was always there to soothe my pain and bring back my confidence.

"You two go into the kitchen. The kettle is boiling and a fire still burning in the grate. I must be off home now. James is waiting for me in the back parlour.

Then she turned to Kate. "What do you think of this young man?"

"You have brought him up well," Kate said.

"It's so true," I put my arms around Nanna. "You have never let me down. You were always there to pick up the pieces. How could I ever have survived without you? And thanks for waiting up for us." I hugged her like I used to do when I was a schoolboy.

"Go on. Stop that. Now you are making me cry again."

"Bless you," she said and silently disappeared, her long skirt swishing across the polished floor.

Chapter 39

I always dreamed of following the Thames to its source. Together Kate and I looked in the guidebook.

"The Thames rises in the Cotswolds and although the source of the Thames is disputed, it is widely accepted to be at Tewkesbury Mead. The stream that flows from Tewkesbury Mead has been called the Thames throughout recorded history," Kate read on. "On its meandering way the Thames flows through the historical towns of Oxford, Abingdon and Henley before passing Windsor Castle and Hampton Court."

We had an early breakfast and Tatters pricked up his ears all set for the adventure. "The picnic basked is all packed and ready," Rosemary said.

It was a clear day as we travelled south on the M5 and make a brief stop along the way to give Tatters a run but didn't delay at the service station. We were just intent on reaching our goal and getting back home before dark. Back on the road again, we discovered it was an easy drive. I concentrated on the busy road ahead and Kate did the navigating.

"The next turn off is Tewkesbury," she said. "We are nearly there." We drove on at a more leisurely pace watching out for more signs.

"There it is," Kate finally said and we drove onto a narrow road leading up into the hills. The final part of the journey was done on foot as we clambered over rocks and moss and Tatters leapt about with great excitement, sniffing at everything as he jumped over rocks and clumps of lichen. It was a moment of intense happiness when we saw the tiny infant Thames babbling like a baby. We dipped our toes in the small, innocent, gurgling brook. It was hard to believe that this was the same river I had come to know and love on the embankment. Tatters ran among the scrub and lapped some water from a tiny pool by the side of the river.

The river can be a wild thing, a dangerous thing prancing and rolling. But this was a quiet river in its infancy, gurgling gently over the rocks.

"Time to make a wish," I said. "My mother had always told me we could make a wish when he visited a place for the first time."

"Close your eyes then," Kate said. She held my hand and we both closed our eyes and made our secret wishes. We walked on for about a further hundred yards and then came upon a plaque. A solitary stone with an inscription.

"This must be it, the source of the great Thames," I said. "At least one of the most likely spots."

We found a flat rock and opened the lunch box. Kate spread the cloth which Rosemary had packed.

"And look at this," she said. "A half bottle of champagne in a cooler bag and two glasses carefully pack in bubble wrap." Kate seemed surprised.

But I had known about that and had my own secret reasons for coming here. I had asked Rosemary to pack the champagne and she looked at me with a twinkle in her eye but didn't ask any questions.

After we had eaten our lunch Kate said, "Will we open the champagne now?"

"Just a minute," I said. I got down on one knee and took Kate's hand. "Kate I have been trying to say this for a long time. Will you marry me? The Thames brought us together and I couldn't think of a better place to ask you. But after all you have been through, I can't blame you if you say no."

"Oh my goodness! What a surprise! No way am I going to say no. In fact, I thought you would never ask," she bent over and kissed me. "This is a relief. In fact I thought I would have to wait for a leap year," she joked. I took the tiny box from my pocket and slipped the sapphire and diamond ring on her finger. "I know this is your birth stone," I said.

She gazed in wonder with tears in her eyes before throwing her arms around me and kissing me again. Then she bent down and produced something from her bag. She opened a small jewellery box and produced a Claddagh gold ring which sparkled in the sunshine.

"I was waiting for this moment and have been going round carrying this in my bag waiting for an appropriate moment to give it to you. You told me once that your grandfather was Irish so I got this for you a long time ago. I think it was after we had been to the Globe."

"It's a most amazing design, quite a masterpiece," I said. "I have seen these rings before and often wondered about the design."

"The ring has a rich tradition with a special history and meaning," Kate explained. "The two hands clasping the heart are a symbol of friendship. The crown means loyalty and of course the heart is a symbol of love. These three qualities are said to combine in a good marriage."

I placed the ring on my left hand with the heart pointing outward. We sat there on a large boulder trying to take it all in.

"There is a story of a Prince who fell in love with a common maid," Kate went on. "He wanted his father to know he was genuine so he designed a ring with hands representing friendship, a crown representing devotion and a heart representing love. He proposed to the girl with the ring and when his father heard the explanation of the symbolism of the ring he gave the son his blessing.

"I like that story but in our case it is the Princess and the Pauper."

"Just one more thing. It is not right for a person to buy a Claddagh ring. They must obtain it as a gift."

"That's really interesting. Thank you, Kate. I will wear it always." We sat with our hands together admiring the rings and the glorious views across the Cotswolds. Tatters jumped up on my knee and licked my face.

"It's his way of saying *Congratulations*," Kate laughed. I wanted time to stand still and enjoy this moment forever.

"This is the happiest moment of my life," I said. "And mine too," Kate agreed and we toasted each other with the champagne."

Kate offered to fill up my glass but I said, "I have got to get you back home safely, all in one piece and we have quite a lot to tell Mother and everyone else."

It had certainly been a day to remember. Back home the dining room was all set for dinner. The table looked even more magnificent that usual with additional flowers and candles. I had hinted to Rosemary that we would like Richard and Louisa to dine with us that night. I wanted them there for the announcement.

But first we went into Mother's sitting room to break the news. "Mother, I want you to be the first person to know that I have asked Kate to marry me. I wanted to do it a long time ago but decided to wait for a time when you could be with us to share in our happiness." We showed her the rings.

"Kevin, I'm pleased for you and Kate. Congratulations!" She put her arms around both of us and held us in a warm embrace. "Now I know why Richard and Louisa are here and the reason for all the fuss in the dining room. James has been running around like a headless chicken with flower arrangements and bottles of wines and spirits. I was beginning to think it was an early Christmas celebration. And by the way I have noticed there are two extra places in the dining room. Rosemary wouldn't give anything away."

"You don't miss much mother," I laughed. "I have invited Rosemary and James to join us for dinner. You know they sometimes join us for special occasions and you could say this is a very special event."

"Oh Kevin, you think of everything. Of course they have to join us. They have been waiting for this day as long as I have."

"And I guess we had better go up to get washed and dressed."

Before we sat down to dinner, I made the announcement.

"I think some of you have already guessed that I have asked Kate to marry me."

"How wonderful, You're a lucky man, Kevin." Richard came over to congratulate us.

"You don't have to remind me," I said. "More than that, I am the luckiest man in the world." I noticed Richard winked at Louisa and I thought it was only a matter of time before they were making their own announcement. There was a lot of kissing and hugging and admiring the rings. Everyone made a wish on the engagement ring which had always been customary in our family.

"Oh my goodness," Rosemary said. Your grandfather had one of those Claddagh rings. It means '*let love and friendship reign*'. Isn't that right?"

"Yes Rosemary, quite right. And I don't have to tell you all those stories. You have known all about the ring for a long time."

"But we want to hear the stories," Louisa said.

"All in good time," I told her. "It's more than just another gold ring."

"And by the way Mother, do you know where granddad's ring went?" I asked.

"No, I'm afraid I don't. Maybe one of his daughters has it. Your aunt Pauline, I suspect."

The celebrations went on well into the night with lots of the best champagne they could find.

"This was waiting for a special occasion," James told us.

"Cheers!" everyone said together. "To Kevin and Kate!"

"I waited day and night for a call, a message or an email," Mother said. "And now here it is, all at once like some sort of miracle. I never thought this day would come."

"It has come eventually Mother and things will be quite different from now on. Believe me."

We sat next to each other and I kissed her hand. "Thank you Mother for being so patient and for being the most wonderful mother in the world. And thanks to Rosemary and James for keeping it all together over the years. And Richard and Louisa. What would life be without such great friends?" There was more champagne, more toasts, more merriment.

"What about a song?" Rosemary asked. "A Christmas Carol or Amazing Grace." Do you remember you sang it at a school concert? It was always my favourite.

No sooner said than done. Kate had already gone to fetch the guitar.

It was strange she asked for that one. Recently I have begun to draw parallels between my own life and that of John Newton, poet and clergyman who had written this song in 1773 from his own experience with the message that forgiveness and redemption are possible regardless of sins committed and that the soul can be delivered from despair.

"Your father used to tell us this story," Rosemary said "about when Newton was a cruel owner of a slave ship and how his spiritual conversion came about when a violent storm battered his vessel so severely that he called out to God for mercy."

"It is without a doubt the most famous of all the folk hymns," James said. "And certainly the most popular in our village church. And you know it has even appeared on popular music charts."

Newton was a self-proclaimed wretch like me who once was lost but then found, saved by some amazing grace. Hadn't I myself been lost and now found? In a way this song sums up my own life too. I tuned up and found a suitable key before singing this most beloved hymn of all time.

"*Amazing grace, how sweet the sound, That saved a wretch like me....*"

"That was your father's favourite hymn too," Rosemary said with tears in her eyes. We all paused for a moment.

I sat there for a brief moment when the song had ended reflecting on my own life. I myself had been a wretch. I had not been enslaved in the sense that Newton had been but had enslaved my own mind and had beaten myself up since Helen's death. I had now begun a spiritual journey although not quite in the religious sense he had done. Newton had been a man of great spiritual stature and humility and his warmth and sincerity shone through. I was not a religious person but I wanted to aspire to even a little of that.

"Hey are you still there?" Richard said.

"Another song," they all demanded.

I moved on and sang a few more of my favourites. Then I adjusted the tuning and said, "This one I'm dedicating to a very special person in my life. I smiled down at Kate who was sitting on the floor at my feet. "This is Kate's song, or rather it is my song for Kate. I tuned the guitar and started the Bette Midler song looking directly to Kate.

"*Some say love, it is a river that drowns the tender reed.*"

I could see a tear running down Kate's face. She had heard me sing it so many times on my busking patch and I knew she loved the lyrics.

"Maybe something more cheerful," I said.

"No, this is my favourite song," Kate pleaded with me to go on. I kept singing....

It's the soul, afraid of dying, that never learns to live.

Now everyone was crying but I had to keep going

When the night has been too lonely, and the road has been too long, And you think that love is only for the lucky and the strong, Just remember in the winter far beneath the bitter snow, Lies a seed, that with the sun's love, in the Spring becomes a rose...."

It was a relief when the song came to an end and I could move on.

"How about a change of mood," I said. "A little birdie has just told me that someone has a birthday today," we all turned towards Rosemary and we sang *Happy Birthday*.

"I couldn't have had a better birthday present," she came over and place her arm around my shoulder. Everyone came around and there was more hugging and birthday wishes. Rosemary requested another song. I tried to choose a couple of more cheerful numbers. The singing continued until I announced that everyone must be sick of my voice.

I looked around the room at the happy faces and thought how lucky I was. "Goodness has a profound way of shining through," I thought.

Chapter 40

There was a lot of emotion as we said our goodbyes at *"Willow Brooks"*.

"But it's not goodbye Mother," I said. "We will be back for the New Year. A big party is planned over at Richards I believe. Fireworks over the river. The lot."

"We have all been invited," Rosemary said, less than two weeks away and I know you two have a lot do in London. I kissed Tatters who was snuggling into mother's arms. "Goodbye. Enjoy your new home!"

"I'll make sure he does. It's the best Christmas gift I have received in years."

We drove slowly down the drive. I watched in the mirror as everyone waved from the doorway. Kate had wound down the window and waved as we rounded the bend. We drove down through the village, out across narrow roads and finally we hit the motorway.

"Our first port of call in London was back at the Shelter to make our announcement and show Maura the rings.

"I was wrong all the time," she said.

"There is an exception to every rule," I reminded her. We stayed for a while talking and laughing with everyone in the dining room. Len was still there expounding on some new theory but he stopped long enough to give us his congratulations.

"We are off now to some Estate Agents in the New Year to choose a place to live, as near the river as possible," I told Maura.

"And I'll be back at the weekends, if you'll have me," Kate said.

"I'll have to think about that," Maura laughed.

"Right then. See you at the engagement party!"

"Thanks for the invitation."

Then we were off making a beeline for the nearest Estate Agent in the area. I read from agent's brochure, "Heavenly retreat.

Exclusive properties have just been refurbished in the idyllic setting of the river Thames."

"Exclusivity, lovely word, isn't it," I said.

"But can we afford it?" Kate asked.

"You don't have to worry about that," I assured her.

"I guess I'll just have to get used to this luxury living," she laughed.

We went to view it. The entrance hall lead directly to a spacious open plan living/dining room with floor to ceiling windows that filled the room with light and drew our attention to the spacious veranda overlooking the river. We held hands as we walked through the living room with its fireplace and recessed lighting.

"The lighting can be designed to be furnished in a number of styles to suit you," the agent said.

Then he led us into the kitchen. "This is the kitchen of distinction like the brochure says. It is fitted with an unparalleled range of appliances. Take your time and have a good look around." After that we were led through to the two master en suite bedrooms with Italian wardrobes and ample storage and mood lighting.

We moved on. "There is also this intimate studio adjacent to the living area suitable for a music room or library. But wait for it," he said moving down a flight of steps. "You have your own private wine cellar, temperature controlled, to keep your most prized vintages."

"I like the sound of that," I said and Kate agreed.

He opened a side door which led to a secure parking space. "And much more," he said quoting the brochure.

"Do we need anything more?" Kate asked.

"I have had more than I could ever have dreamed of," I put my arm around her shoulder and we had one last look across the river.

Looking at the wonderful views, I realised that this was the place I had always dreamed of, the quiet seclusion, the lovely natural setting on the river and the London Eye in the distance. I now had London in my blood.

We thanked the agent and told him we would meet him back at the office. The deal was struck. It was only a matter of going through the conveyancing process.

"There is no onward chain so there will be no delays," we were told.

After the viewing, Kate said, "Now it's time for my treat. You buy the house and I buy the afternoon tea," she laughed giving me the greatest bear hug.

We walked along the south bank past the London Eye for traditional afternoon tea in the exclusive hotel.

"This is the life," I said as we sat indulging in home-baked scones, fresh strawberry preserves, clotted cream, a selection of tea, pastries and sandwiches, with unrivalled views across the Thames overlooking the Palace of Westminster, Big Ben and the Eye. It was the end of another perfect day.

The next day we made arrangements for the Engagement party and sat together writing out the invitations to our families, Kate's colleagues and their partners, Richard and Louisa and a small group of my friends. Maura and Sr. Gabriel were also on the list which seemed to be growing by the minute.

"Surely Sr. Gabriel won't want to come to a wine tasting venue," I said.

"You must be joking," Kate said. "What do you bet? Hers will be the first reply we receive." And it was.

It was Christmas 2006 and only a matter of time waiting for the negotiations for the completion of the purchase of our new property. In the meantime Kate had moved into my apartment. I was having the best Christmas for a long time. I had something to celebrate. I had Kate. This year was different. It was going to be his happiest Christmas ever. Together Kate and I started to make plans, drove down to Rotherhithe to choose a Christmas tree. It wasn't going to be an enormous one and when we spotted a little lopsided tree in the corner we knew it was perfect for our small living room.

We tied it on the roof of the car in a precarious position. Kate took responsibility for the decorations and together we sipped champagne and put the angel on top of our little tree. At last the finishing touches were in place and we did a general tidy up before our friends arrived for an early Christmas drink. We walked up to St. Martin in the Fields in Trafalgar Square for the Christmas service and smiled at the enormity of the tree near the high altar.

As the organ boomed out the final Christmas carol, Kate held my hand tightly we had walked out into the cold evening. It was the first fall of snow and wrapped up warmly we walked hand in hand down the south bank. Richard had secured a 'not guilty' verdict for Mahmud and this had been one of the best Christmas presents we could have had.

We drove down to Kate's parents for Christmas lunch where we received a warm welcome, more champagne, exchanging of gifts and talking about plans for the future. For a moment I stood in silence, overcome by my own happiness

Chapter 41

It was the evening of the engagement party and we walked down the south bank towards London Bridge and found Vinopolis which created a truly stylish extravaganza under the stunning old Victorian railway arches. As Kate predicted Sr. Gabriel was one of the first to arrive.

When everyone else had gathered, we started with a glass of wine and then spent the afternoon sampling wines from around the world. There was a guided wine-tasting tour for our engagement party.

"Glory be to God. I could get used to this," Sr. Gabriel said.

"I do believe you are a little tipsy," Kate laughed.

"Call me Gabby. Everyone else does," Sr. Gabriel said. "And whatever you do don't tell Reverend Mother that I had one too many."

"I'm sure she would be glad to see you letting your hair down. You work so hard," Kate said.

"You must be joking. You don't know Reverend Mother.

Sr. Gabriel wasn't the only one to be merry. The mixture of wines was beginning to take its toll. When we eventually got to the dining room, we all had a drop too much. Kate sat opposite me and leaned across the table.

"Do you remember the first time we met, or I should say the first time you decided to speak to me, you asked me if I believed in fate. I gave some sort of vague answer but now I know the answer is yes. I had not gone to the Shelter to find a husband but fate has been kind to me."

"It's certainly the last place on earth to find one," Pauline said.

By now they were all in high spirits after their wine sampling. Their inhibitions had gone. After the meal the men had settled in their own favourite position near the bar.

"How do you become a volunteer at the Shelter?" Beki asked.

"Are there any more Kevins?" Trish wanted to know and they all giggled.

"There are no more Kevins anywhere else in the world." Kate said.

"Oh Kate we are so happy for you," Pauline said. "When is the big day?"

"Don't worry you'll all be getting invitations. Nothing is confirmed yet but it will be around Valentine's Day. We need to book the Church. We would like the children's school choir to sing at our wedding. Do you think that will be allowed?" Kate asked Pauline.

"I don't see why not. We will start practising straight away. Just give us a list of the hymns," Pauline said.

"But Kevin wants some traditional church music, I mean as well as the children's choir."

"I thought you said he wasn't a religious person," Beki looked up in surprise, still a bit giggly and not taking anything too seriously.

"I'm still not sure about that but he likes class and traditional things."

"Oh dear we had better get up there to Harvey Nicholls and buy our wedding outfits," Christine joked.

"It's the best night I have had in a long time," Sr. Gabriel said as we all said goodnight and went our separate ways. "Let's hope Reverend Mother is asleep when I get in. I have a key to the side door and if I take off my shoes no one will be any the wiser." We put her in a taxi and off she went beaming from ear to ear and waving to everyone through the window.

As we walked back up the South Bank, Kate said, "I wonder when we will get the keys of our new house. I can't wait. My Dad has been talking about hiring a van to remove our stuff and Richard has agreed to give you both a hand. I can pack all the small things and it shouldn't take all that long. It's not as though was have a massive amount of furniture."

Chapter 42

The day we moved in was one of those rare moments when nature had conspired to create the perfect moment in my life. The sky turned a deep pink which appeared to be the setting for a thunderstorm. But the rain lessened and the most perfect rainbow arched across the sky, over the Eye, across the river and over the dome of St Pauls. There was a bolt of lightning in the distance. This spectacular sky seemed to be in harmony with my elated feelings of happiness.

"This was the most important journey of my life and I have made it with you," I said as we stood on the balcony, Kate leaned lightly on my arm.

"This is something special," she said. "I have never seen anything like it and I am sure that someone up there is rejoicing in our happiness." Spectrums of light spread across the river. The storm ended and when I gazed up I saw Jock's star and the brightness of the golden dome stood against the darkening sky. Life had been generous.

At last I felt safe and contented. I was fortunate enough to meet some exceptional human beings. They had given me so much and had such an impact on my life. They had helped me to survive despite incredibly difficult odds. I was so deliriously happy and had learned a new language, a language of enthusiasm. Of things accomplished with love and purpose. I had found hidden treasures once the initial obstacles had been overcome.

"If we strive to become better than we are, everything around us becomes better too," Maura said. She believed in positivity. "Stop feeling guilty and sorry for yourself. Try to open your mind and your heart to a new way of thinking and living." I had done all of that, eradicated the fear and guilt from my life. I had learned to love myself enough to forgive myself. After careful consideration and soul searching, I was ready to face any new challenges. My heart had begun to soar. The world could be mine again.

"Look what is in front of you. Not what is behind you? Give the world a chance to support you," Maura had said. "Life's secrets are unfathomable." I began to challenge myself and accept responsibility for my future, for my life and behaviour. Life is short and Kate had made it sweeter. All my tears turned into joy.

"I thought the sun would never shine again, but you have given me life, higher than the soul can hope." I told Kate as we looked across the wide expanse of water to where the London Eye kept turning. The sky was a palette of many colours.

Strangely some of the most rewarding days were those I had spent on the streets. It gave me an opportunity to see my whole life and the whole world in perspective, like time spent in the wilderness on a sort of pilgrimage.

"This is the happiest moment of my life," I said.

I would never leave the shadow of the Eye. It had been a beacon for me and Kate had been my anchor and my sail. She had steered me through some stormy seas and now we had reached our haven.

"You have brought me to this day and this retreat away from the choppy waters of my guilty past."

"You brought yourself to this day," Kate said as she placed her arm around my shoulder. It was a dream come true.

I had learned the secret of happiness. "Where your heart is, there is your treasure." Kate had transformed me. She made my life worth living. I had conquered my own negativity and I was going back to the life I knew.

I thought back to my early days on the street when I had stood still, looking grim, ill at ease, my hair streaming, soaked to the bone in my shabby pullover, shivering with cold. This was the punishment for my own guilt? I looked back at those two years not with anger but with compassion and insights, full of the strange atmosphere of an intersection between the real and the unreal.

I would give Kate a good life. We would face obstacles together instead of running away from them. Being with her made me feel in control of my life. It was something about being free to do what I wanted to do and I knew that together we could face any challenge. I can almost see it, almost hear it now, like music in my mind, a new life, a new hope, a place beyond my wildest dreams.

This was the finest moment of my life. From now on it would be all downhill. I put my arms around Kate and held her close. "I'm going to remember this moment for the rest of my life," Kate said.

"There is no doubting the fact that our relationship was written the stars," I looked across at the setting sun, flaming red over the dome of St. Paul's Cathedral.

But just then there was a loud knock on the door which made Kate start. "Are we expecting someone?" she asked.

"Not that I know of," I shrugged my shoulders and walked towards the front door.

Out on the doorstep, a figure draped in a long black coat, gazed up and down the front of the building, tapped thin fingers impatiently on the glass panel on the side of the door and placed his hand back on the knocker.

Lightning Source UK Ltd.
Milton Keynes UK
UKOW05f1819131114

241574UK00001B/9/P